Digital
Forensic
Diaries

Mike Sheward

© 2014-2017 Mike Sheward
www.digitalforensicdiaries.com
Enquiries: mail@secureowl.com
ISBN: 9781521514467

Preface

I have been fortunate enough to work in a field that I really enjoy for several years now. For the small segment of its history that I've been involved in the information security industry, I have seen considerable growth. People are waking up to the fact that the safety and security of data is of vital importance in today's connected economy.

A few years ago, I decided to write these stories to share with a wider audience the true face of one of the most fascinating sub areas of information security, digital forensics.

I hate to break it to you; digital forensics is not as it is portrayed in television and film. There are no magical programs that can decrypt heavily encrypted data within a few seconds behind some fancy graphics, while a ridiculously good-looking investigator watches on.

The good news is that digital forensics doesn't need to be portrayed this way to be interesting. In real life, the stories of incidents and how investigators untangle them are often much more interesting than the same old stories peddled on the TV. The problem of course, is that for confidentially reasons; those stories are hardly ever shared.

In these stories, I've drawn on real life experiences to create tales that hopefully do justice to the field of digital forensics.

Although the industries, names and settings have changed to protect those who have trusted me to be a part of their investigations, the tools, techniques and incidents described are all very real examples of things that happen every single day in this line of work.

I hope you enjoy reading them.

Also, I am not Parker Foss; he is a much-improved version of me. He always knows the exact correct thing to say, knows exactly where to look and probably drives a better car than I do.

Bastard.

For Jessica and Oliver.

Table of Contents

Introduction

My name is Parker Foss, and I am a digital forensics investigator and security tester. Digital forensics is both a scientific and artistic process. I investigate computer security incidents on behalf of my varied and always interesting client base. I don't advertise.

Looking back through my case notes, I've recreated the stories of some of my favourite investigations for your enjoyment.

Oh, one more thing, information security and digital forensics are the most interesting subjects on the planet; I just hope that I do these topics justice in my own work.

Racing for Answers

Racing for Answers: Chapter One

The afternoon sun painted never-ending shadows across the pristine asphalt, while simultaneously illuminating the red and yellow advertising hoardings promoting various tyre and oil suppliers. The air was thick with the smell of 'higher than normal' octane petrol, and a minor earthquake occurred each time an engine was fired up.

I was being escorted by Dave Simmonds, who was the Chief Legal Officer for one of the top five motor racing teams in the world, XT Racing. In a world where your competitors closely scrutinise every action you take, his principle task du jour was to prevent anyone aside from a select few members of his own team knowing who I was. He'd barely spoken a word to me since we'd met at the paddock entrance. I headed round a maze formed out of stacks of tyres in various states of ware, and found myself in a rather lavish motorhome.

For corporate guests, Mimosas were on offer at the entrance. I was not a guest, not yet anyway – maybe if I did a good job here one day I'd be invited back. For now, at least, that role was reserved for a bunch of Rolex sporting, 'Yves Saint Ralph Lauren' smelling, fake tanned tosspots. Oh, how I longed to be a tosspot.

A sliding glass door opened with a soft whizzing sound and I found myself on the bridge of the Starship enterprise, or a private conference room, whichever works.

Dave finally spoke sentences to me. It turned out he was Scottish.

"I appreciate you getting here at such short notice, but this is a particularly sensitive matter and we need this dealt with ASAP", he said. "The executive team has put aside some funding for the type of work you do, but it is not an unlimited amount, so we hope that you discover something in the short window of time you'll have to spend working with us".

"Well, I am glad that I can be of service, and I'll certainly try and find the answers you are looking for" I replied while smiling, Dave did not smile back, he just looked at me. I figured he was trying to work out if I was trustworthy or if my 'fan boy' status would impact my ability to keep what I was doing a secret.

As was fairly typical, I didn't really have a clue as to the specifics of the investigation or testing I was about to conduct. However, given that my initial meeting was with the Chief Legal Officer, I assumed I would need to reach for my write blockers, rather than fire up Burpsuite Pro. I tried to act like I'd been here a million times before, which was true to an extent, this wasn't going to be my first forensics rodeo, but it was the first one that I'd have done at a race track.

"So, what are we dealing with, someone been downloading porn in the pit lane, stealing secrets and selling them to another team, sending abusive emails to your team manager?" I asked, hoping that my one of my multiple-choice options fit the bill for what I was about to get into.

"I'm afraid it is not as cut and dry as that". "I'm assuming from your giddiness as we walked in, you are a fan of the sport?" Dave asked. I nodded in response, but wasn't quite sure why it was relevant. I was also pissed off that I'd shown 'giddiness'. I didn't really think I had, I hadn't run around screaming through the paddock and started asking for autographs from the three or four folks I'd recognised off of the telly.

"So, you'll be aware that so far this year, our car has been, shall we say, a piece of shit?" I was happy that Dave had taken us across the shit barrier. I always like it when a client starts to swear, because that means I no longer have to be on my guard about trying not to swear myself.

"Trouble is, no one can quite figure out why – and it really shouldn't be this way. We've invested more time and funding into this year's car than any other team in history". At this point, I began to think that he should have probably called an aerodynamicist or a mechanic, and I guess Dave noticed the 'what the crap does that have to do with me' look starting to emerge on my face because he addressed this point without my prompting.

"So, in case you are wondering why we called you. At this point, have investigated every angle. The aero, the engine, the gearbox, the turbo, even redesigned the frigging rear view mirrors – and still nothing. The car still slows down like a piece of shit during the race."

"Ah yes, but you have been doing pretty well in qualifying" I piped up, showing at least some contextual knowledge.

"Correct" Dave replied, "but unfortunately sponsors don't care about qualifying, and there is no prize money for qualifying well. The world's best drivers aren't happy unless you give them a car that is capable of winning the races." Dave wasn't wrong; his team employed two former world champions as drivers, with salaries in the millions of dollars. They were quick blokes.

"Our Chief Engineer has been in this sport for twenty-five years. He has never seen the types of problems that we've had this year during the races…" Dave glanced to check one more time that the door was shut. "The only area we haven't investigated is sabotage."

"Mmm… interesting, so you think someone on the team is doing something to sabotage your races?" I got out my notepad and started to jot down my first impressions. I always did this in the moment, because you never know what minor observation might allow you to put two and two together later on. Dave nodded, and began to elaborate on his suspicions.

"There aren't many folk on the team with a motivation to make us lose, all the technical staff get paid pretty nice bonuses if we win. As do the drivers. However, considering what we are seeing, it remains a possibility and I want to rule it out."

"Okay, makes sense." Dave spun a non-disclosure agreement towards me, and indicated I should sign it. This was common practice, so I had no hesitation.

"What I'd like to do, is provide you with full access to our datacentre and all of our internal computer systems – both engineering and corporate. I want you to look through everything to find any indication from anyone that they may be under duress, or otherwise involved in an arrangement to sabotage our cars prior to a race."

"Understood" I murmured while continuing to jot notes down.

"Now, the reason I've asked you to join us here at the track, is that the full race team is here." Dave checked the door again; he really didn't want anyone to walk in on us. "If anyone is doing something to these cars before the race, then they'll be here." Dave stood up. "I want you to learn the names of the guys, and look at the trackside systems they are using. Everything is in scope. If you need access to something, come to me, and I'll find a way to get you that access while alerting as few people as possible". Dave's attitude was most welcome, sometimes folks are hesitant to let you fully into their systems, making the job trickier, or forcing you to waste hours while waiting on the right person to approve and grant access. No such problems here, it seemed.

Dave then explained to me how he'd already briefed the garage that there would be a new face walking round. I was an IT Consultant, who'd want to know about the systems the team were using to understand better how they could be optimized for improved performance while further away from base. I was asked to change out of my 'suit-suit' into a fireproof suit, regulations for anyone in the pit lane. We walked together across the paddock to the team garage, where a crew of about 35 people was working on various bits of the car. These folks were referred to as the 'race team', and travelled around the world with the team to about twenty different events a year. Back at the factory, which was only about forty miles down the road from the track that was hosting this weekend's race, a further three hundred people were employed. Everything including painters, model makers, scientists and software engineers were on the payroll. This was serious business, with big money at stake. Fractions of a second in lap time could make hundreds of millions of dollars worth of difference in prize money.

I had briefly chatted with Dave about performing an offline seizure of the team's email servers. They hosted an on-premise email solution in the factory, and steps were being taken to provide me with a disk image from the email server overnight. Indeed, while I was in the garage I overheard some of the crew moaning that IT was taking email down for a couple of hour's overnight.

"Why the eff would they do that on a race weekend? Dickheads!" said one heavily tattooed mechanic.

I spent the next few hours observing the team at work, and spoke with a few of the guys. I learned pretty quickly that they had two distinct networks. The corporate network, which every team employee had access to. This network hosted things like email, intranet sites, file shares and document repositories. The team public website was also hosted internally from this network.

The second network was known as the engineering network, and it was segregated from the corporate network by a firewall. Access was much more strictly controlled, but remote access was possible. Only those with a need were allowed access to engineering. This network included systems that controlled machines used to manufacture parts, massive computing arrays that performed computational fluid dynamics, and telemetry systems that received data from the cars.

I asked one of the crew if the drivers had access to the engineering network, more out of interest than anything else. Although a driver was considered a member of the engineering team, they were so high profile I figured they'd probably be a likely target for someone looking to crack into the team's systems; so, limiting their access might be a smart move. I found out that one of the drivers had this access, while the other did not. The reason for the discrepancy was explained to me. One driver had been a former member of the XT Racing development driver program, whereas the other one, without the access, had been signed directly from another team. As a development driver, Aaron Shelley had sat with the race team in the garage for the first two years of his career, so that he could be prepared for the challenge of racing at this level. During this time, he'd worked on engineering systems, reviewing data that he could later use to understand how to drive the car, hence the access.

Although it seemed unlikely, a driver was a potential candidate for sabotage. They, after all, had more one on one time with the car than anyone else, and they, could of course, just slow down during the race. I discussed this possibility with Dave.

"It would be near impossible for a driver to drive slowly on purpose, and for it not to be detected by the crew" he explained. "I'm not an expert on these systems by

any means, but I do know that telemetry would show a driver lifting off the throttle, and that would be raised as an issue right away."

As a fan of the sport, I agreed with Dave. It does seem counterproductive for a driver, whose entire purpose in life is to be the fastest, to slow down. As an investigator however, I didn't discount the possibility completely. Digital forensics work often places you in a void between computer science and psychology. Humans do crazy things for crazy reasons, and racing drivers, although they will never admit it, are human after all.

I spent the rest of my time with the race team learning more about the systems in use, and gathering various names. The cars came back in from several hours of practice time, and they were promptly wrapped up in what appeared to be a car shaped body bag. One hour after the cars had returned, all computer systems were powered off, and all personnel left the garage, including me.

"Parc ferme rules" Dave explained as he walked me out of the paddock. "The governing body decided that cars can't be touched by anyone between the sessions, means you have to use the same set up to qualify, as you do to race." I stopped, and looked at Dave.

18

"Well, how is that enforced?" I asked. "How do the governing body make sure that no one from the team touches the cars?"

Dave explained that the governing body managed a CCTV system, which recorded all garage action during times the parc ferme rules were in place. In addition, a curfew prevented team staff from working in the garage past a specific time, without a special permission and monitoring from the governing body.

"So, what opportunity would someone have to sabotage the cars prior to the race then, given the parc ferme rules?"

"Very little opportunity indeed, for one person acting alone." Dave replied.

I nodded my head in agreement; perhaps I was now looking for multiple suspects.

I bid farewell to Dave at the paddock entrance.

"Oh, one more thing..." he said as I turned away. "If this is really happening, whoever is doing it, is able to cover it up so well, that the team can't detect it after the race."

"Mmm...so to recap, I'm looking for electronic evidence of potential sabotage, where there is no motive that we know of, very little opportunity to do it, and no physical evidence either."

"You got it," he said. "You'll really earn your frigging money if you can figure this one out."

He wasn't kidding.

Racing for Answers: Chapter Two

The next morning, I drove to the team's factory. It wasn't a traditional factory by any means, there were no chimneys pumping out smoke while droves of soot-covered workers marched in. It looked more like a tech company headquarters, with a fountain and glass frontage. It was all extremely clean.

With the race team still at the track, I figured it'd be a great opportunity to take a look around the on-site datacentre, and see some of the back-end hardware that could hold the key to this investigation. I also collected the email server image that had been prepared for me overnight from a local point of contact.

To my surprise, the factory was packed. It turned out that for every person in the race team at the track of a weekend, there were three or four back at the factory watching systems in even more detail. Reprising my legend as a performance consultant, I visited the racing operations centre, a room with three rows of folks sat around in semicircle looking at several large monitors. The monitors showed lived performance data from the cars, as well as TV coverage of the race.

I sat at an empty seat on the back row, and introduced myself to an employee on the back row. She was a design engineer, responsible for the gearbox. I introduced myself and she reciprocated. Her name was Janet Alexia, and she'd been with the team for two years. She was more than willing to explain what she was looking at on her screen. Essentially, she was studying the live data from about a dozen sensors on the gearbox of each XT Racing car, and making notes about how it was affecting the performance.

I spoke with a couple more folks throughout the day, including a software engineer, who'd worked on what he'd referred to as the car's on-board operating system. This OS was operated by the drivers' inputs to the thirty or so buttons and dials on the steering wheel. It turned out that every team wrote their own OS for the car, but the governing body delivered a standard engine control unit, or ECU, to the teams. The ECU had software on it, which could not be modified by anyone other than the governing body. Each time the governing body produced new ECU software; they'd make the version available to all teams. They'd also produce an MD5 hash for each version, and as part of scrutineering after the race; they'd check the MD5 hash to make sure that the software hadn't been tampered with. I added this to my notes; I was quite impressed to see this level of diligence in the sport.

My final conversation took place in a private room, with someone who knew exactly who I was and why I was at the factory. He was the IT manager and had actually been my point of contact for the email system image. We mutually agreed on some logs that would be of use to my investigation, including access logs for the engineering network for the past few months. He also gave me an overview of their Active Directory structure, and procedures in place regarding hires and terminations, specifically making sure that people who had left the team no longer had access. The team had a fairly vigorous security program in place, the main objective of which was to secure access to sensitive design data. A few years earlier, there had been a widely-publicised case in another team of a designer supplying information to a rival. XT were keen for that not to happen to them. After all, they spent millions trying to be the fastest, why should someone else benefit from their investment.

I left the factory with all requisite chain of custody documentation completed and headed to my lab. It was late, and the weekend, but I had wanted to get the disk image processing overnight so that I could start digging through its contents as soon as possible.

Although I'd been at the factory all day, it suddenly occurred to me that I wasn't fully aware of how that day's race had gone. I'd been so involved in the details of the systems I'd studied, that the actual goings on in the race had escaped me. I flicked on the sports radio station and listened. After twenty minutes of football scores, they finally mentioned the race. XT had not won. After leading for most of the race, they had lost time in the middle stint between pit stops. Aaron Shelley had finished sixth, and his teammate, had only just been able to finish the race in fifteenth due to overheating problems. Shelley was interviewed, and bemoaned the cars lack of pace during the middle stint. The team principal was next to be interviewed, and he reiterated his desire for his team to get to the bottom of their woes.

It occurred to me that I should call Dave Simmonds, to see if anything had been found during the post-race study of the car. I did so via my hands-free kit, and he was able to tell me pretty quickly that once again, they had been unable to locate any issues with the car following the race. I updated him with my next steps and promised to call if anything came up.

Back at the lab I set the disk image up to process in our distributed processing system. This system takes a disk image, and indexes all of the contents of that image, including data that has been deleted for easy analysis and investigation. That process can take a very long time, hence why it is usually something we leave running overnight. While that process got started, I opened up the access logs provided by the IT manager to examine the format. It was pretty straightforward, UTC access time, source IP address, and username. I also had a list of current usernames, and the team employee they represented.

I wrote a quick python script that parsed the IP address entries out of the logs, and added a couple more pieces of information to the log file. First of all, the country the IP address was based in, secondly the Internet service provider or organisation that owned the IP. There were quite a few entries in the log, and the geo-location and ownership data was being pulled from an online service via a rate limited API, so I decided, after a couple of sanity checks, to let this run overnight also.

This point in any investigation is probably my favourite. The investigation is so new that my head is bubbling with possibilities. So many angles to look at, so much fresh data that could hold the key to making a significant discovery. All this before reaching the point of having spent a few days going over the data time and time again, with the stale data not offering any new leads, and driving me insane. I despise investigations that go stale, so I try to prevent that from happening, by collecting only a narrow slice of data where possible. I headed home, safe in the knowledge that while the lab computers were busy churning away overnight, my head wouldn't be far behind them, and sleep would be tricky.

I was awoken the next morning by a text message that'd I requested. It was twenty to six, and the processing software had sent an automated message saying it had finished its initial sift of the disk image. This system has a habit of texting at weird hours, and my wife often joked that she'd be happier if I was getting text messages from other women, if they were to arrive at more sociable hours.

I arrived at the lab, coffee in hand, ready to start digging. I began performing keyword searches against the image. I decided to start with the word 'sabotage', on the off chance that I'd find something. It was highly unlikely that anyone involved in a sophisticated sabotage campaign would send an email from their team email account to their buddy saying, 'hey, I just sabotaged the car, lol' but you'd never know unless you looked. Stranger things have happened. In this case no luck, just a couple of innocent conversations, wordlists and dictionaries.

One thing that was telling from that particular keyword search was the lack of any internal email conversations between Dave Simmonds and anyone else about the hiring of me to investigate potential sabotage. This really was something they were doing on the down low.

I tried a few other words and phrases. Things like 'make them lose', 'make us lose', 'losing', 'technical problem', 'payments', 'disrupt' and 'damage', I then spent a good four or five hours following several email trails that lead to nowhere interesting. Next on my agenda was to search the emails for any encrypted attachments that may have been indicative of some clandestine communications. There were about three dozen such files, but many seemed from the nature of the recipient to be sponsorship contract and design information, which I would have expected to be transmitted encrypted in any case.

Sometimes when working on this type of case, you get lost in the detail, when really you need to take a step back and look at the bigger picture. So, to that end, an exercise I like to do, is to create visualisations from the data I have that could help me spot irregularities and outliers. This is usually something I do on firewall logs to spot intrusions, but I figured this might be a good time to try and put this to practice on the email data I had. I extracted all email sender, recipient and subject information, as well as timestamps and dropped them into a CSV file. Opening up a visualisation tool, I produced charts and statistics that I hoped would lead me down the correct path. Some questions I asked of my data were: who sends the most emails from XT? What does typical day's worth of email traffic look like? Which sender and recipient pairs produce the highest amount of email chatter? What types of attachments are being sent out, and by whom?

I had the answers to these questions pretty quickly, but those answers alone are just quantitative statistics. Although useful, they do little for me in understanding the human elements at play. So, to add context, I dropped in from my employee name file, information such as the sender and recipient's respective department name and job title. To give an example of why this was so useful, I could see there was a high amount of chatter between a couple of employees who given their job titles, probably wouldn't have had a need to talk to each all that much, so I looked into it. However, after a quick read, I could see that they were in fact married, and most of their emails were 'I'm going to lunch, coming down to join me?'

My attention was drawn to a sender recipient pair, who had a particularly high frequency of emails for about two weeks about 3 months previously, before the chatter had suddenly stopped. One of the pair I knew I'd met previously. It was the software engineer, who had written the operating system installed on the car. The second name in that pair wasn't familiar to me, and hadn't resolved against the employee list, which lead me to believe that this person wasn't an employee any longer. It wasn't hard to decipher the real human name behind the email alias, so I decided to search online to see if I could find what role that person had at the team. It didn't take me long to find out. The name was Sergjei Utkin, and until about 3 months ago, he'd been a development driver with XT. The same program that Aaron Shelley had been a part of. However, unlike Shelley, XT decided that Utkin just wasn't cutting it, and decided that they didn't want to continue his involvement in the development program.

I found this to be an interesting discovery and noted it down. It wasn't just the high volume of the email exchanges between Utkin and the engineer that made me take note. It became apparent that they'd become quite good friends, and most of the emails were social in nature. There did not seem to be anything malicious in any of the content, but, here you have one guy who now has a motivation to be mad at the team, being dropped unceremoniously from a potentially lucrative development scheme, and his buddy, who just so happened to write the software for the car.

Although I considered this an interesting discovery, it was far from being a 'smoking gun'. After all, this engineer wasn't part of the race team, and wouldn't have had the opportunity to physically sabotage the car. He wasn't the only engineer working on the OS either; there was a QA process in place for the software. A team of about six developers all had access to the source code repository, and a totally different team did the QA work and shipped the code to 'production', which in this case was the race cars on-board computers. It did open my mind to a completely new idea though, could the cars operating system be sabotaged? That was a question I couldn't answer. I'd need to go back at talk with the team; I added this to my list of follow up questions.

I found nothing else of value in my search of the emails, so decided to switch my attention to my engineering network access log. The same analytical principles applied here. I charted out the data to help me get a visual on the who, where and how often folks accessed the network. The majority of the remote access was sourced from a satellite broadband provider, who I figured were responsible for the team's remote communications while they were on the road.

I was also able to map out remote access from various countries during timeframes that matched perfectly with the race and test calendar I downloaded from the Internet. It seemed that team members carried on working from their hotels when they left the circuit.

I found one outlier in the access log that sparked my interest. It was a login to Aaron Shelley, the race driver's account, which had occurred while the team was in Spain for a pre-season test. What made it an outlier was that the source IP address was different to the rest of the team members. The last octet was a few digits higher. I traced the IP back to the same satellite broadband provider, and reasoned that it could just have been part of a load-balancing configuration or that he'd logged in via a system that was configured differently, but that IP address never appeared in the logs again.

I checked out that ISP's website to see if I could understand the technology in play. I found out that the ISP was also a provider to another team in the same racing series, and they weren't shy about boasting about the partnership. I couldn't find much out that would explain why one login from their network for the same customer would be sourced from a different IP, so I added it to my follow up questions, and planned on posing it to the IT manager.

At the end of the day I'd pulled an interesting couple of leads, but absolutely nothing concrete. I'd hoped to be able to give something more valuable to Dave during our update call than the shocking revelation two of his employees were friends, and one strange IP address in a log file that he probably wouldn't really understand all that much. I guess I could try express the investigation in sporting terms he'd understand, 'it's a marathon, not a sprint!'

Racing for Answers: Chapter Three

After our update call, Dave had requested that I join him at the factory. He'd promised to arrange meetings with the relevant folks to answer the questions I'd had in regards to the satellite broadband IP address, and also the possibility that the cars operating system could have been sabotaged. Overall, he'd been pleasantly surprised that I'd come back with follow up questions so quickly.

"I was expecting a boat load of nothing, so at least now I know that you've at least been looking" he'd said during our call. Nothing like a vote of confidence from your customers!

I met with Dave in his office where the senior manager of the software development group joined us.

"So, you think someone is adding dodgy lines of code to our software do you? Well, to be honest mate, that is a pretty crazy accusation right there". I hadn't even been properly introduced to the guy yet, but already he was defensive. Nothing unusual about that, anytime you turn up at someone's place of work as an outsider, and suggest that they might be responsible for a team that screwed up; it tends to go down like a lead balloon.

"Well…" I began, "I want to know if it is a feasible at least. I'm not an expert by any stretch of the imagination on embedded racing car operating systems, so I'd like your help. You are the expert; do you think it's a possibility?"

I always found that calling someone an expert calmed him or her down. Unless you were calling them an expert wanker of course, which I'd been known to do from time to time.

I could tell the guy was hesitant to give an answer. I think in his heart of hearts he knew that it probably would be possible for someone to sneak a line or two of code into the software, but at the same time he believed in his guys and their process, and had serious doubts that they'd get away with it if they tried. I asked to go take him for a coffee to discuss this in more detail. Dave had other matters to attend to; so would not be joining us. On our way out of the office, Dave had one more piece of information for me.

"Oh, by the way. On your I.P. address question, they say they have no explanation for the different address, apparently, each customer has a different one." Dave really stressed the 'I' and the 'P', like he really didn't know what one was, which was fine, it just made me chuckle inside. I thanked Dave for the info and carried on heading out for coffee with my slightly tamed development manager. I let Dave's statement about the IP address register in the back of my mind, but didn't really think too much more about it. I was busy prepping questions in my head about the operating system.

It turned out; the development manager had a name, Keith Hartwell, and after a few minutes of chatting with him one on one, he loosened up a bit. He gave me the run down on the operating system his team had produced. It was a custom spin of a well-known lightweight Linux distribution. Some components of the distribution had been removed; many others were produced in house. The majority of code used was written in C, but there were other languages in use. The release cycle for the software was in line with the race calendar. A new version was delivered, QA'ed and installed a few days before each race weekend.

Keith confirmed what I'd been told previously by his engineer. There were a team of six working on all the code, and they had a separate team who actually performed installation on the cars. The build was installed on the car over a USB cable directly connected to the race team electrical engineer's laptop.

I asked if was possible to download the build from the car, as opposed to upload. Keith confirmed that it would be, and so I suggested a simple test we could perform to ensure the integrity of the build.

"Firstly, we get a copy of the package from the source code repository that was applied to the car prior to the last race. I'll generate a hash of that build. Next, we'll pull down the package from the car, providing it was the same version used in the last race. Run a hash on that copy and compare the two. If they are the same we'll know that we have two exact copies of the build." I explained to Keith. "We'll then do a deep dive review of the code to look for anything untoward. I may need your help with this bit."

Keith agreed to the plan, and scrambled to have the relevant folks pull the build from a car before it was overwritten. That said, the team didn't want me to take their software out of the factory, so they set me up with a desk in a quiet part of the factory where I could perform my analysis. The packages were pretty small files; only about seven hundred megs each, so obtaining and hashing them didn't take very long.

"Well, what's the verdict?" Keith asked over my shoulder.

"The hashes match. This code is exactly what is installed on the car, let's get digging." Keith nodded and we started to peruse the files in the build. We spent hours poring over lines and lines of code. This happened mostly in silence, with me occasionally asking Keith questions about the purpose of the odd line of code or function. After many hours, we came to a conclusion. There was nothing in the operating system that shouldn't have been there. The code was clean, and I had wasted an entire day of this poor bloke's time. Fortunately, I think Keith's relief outweighed his frustration.

So, where next, I thought to myself. I began to question whether I'd ever work this one out, and also wondered how much credibility I'd lost by suggesting something as 'out there' as tampered software selectively breaking a racing car. Keith was about to leave, and I knew I'd probably have trouble getting his co-operation again anytime soon, so I looked down my notebook for anything that I'd written down that I could possibly follow up on before he got out the door. I remembered a code block that had been commented out, that had a note associated with it that I wanted to seek clarity on. The comments related to a function in the code called P2CA, and read 'disabling P2CA per the 2014 regs'. I asked Keith what P2CA was, and why it had been disabled.

"P2CA stands for Pit to Car Adjustments, it was a technology we used to use to send dynamic updates to engine maps and other parameter changes to the car during the race, remotely from the pits."

"Wow, that's pretty smart, so if something is going wrong with the car, you could fix it remotely?" I replied.

"Exactly, that was the plan, however the governing body banned that function for this year, so we had to disable it. I guess we just commented out the code block that allowed it to function. The technical manager is trying to persuade them to allow us to turn this back on next year. Plus, we may still have some components in the overall code module that we use for our traditional one way, car to pit reporting telemetry."

I then started to press Keith for more information about how the car and the pit communication worked. I could see from the code that it seemed like the connection back to the pit was operating over a normal TCP/IP connection, just like a regular wireless device such as a phone or tablet.

"Yep" said Keith, "it is probably one of the most expensive wireless devices ever created! Using a satellite connection, it creates a certificate authenticated VPN tunnel back to our engineering network. This is how we get real time telemetry, and this setup is more secure and reliable than sending via radio like we used to."

"So, when the car is on, and sending data back, it has an IP address on the engineering network, like any other client machine?" I enquired. The answer was yes.

"Any firewalls restricting the ports that can be accessed on that IP?" The answer to this question was a big fat no.

I found that to be quite fascinating, anyone on the engineering network had the ability to talk directly to the car via its IP while it was operational. By design, the teams code would only send certain data one way, however, if any additional ports were open on the operating system, SSH for example, there could be away to gain access to the underlying Linux build. This opened up a whole new line of questioning, and I really needed to dig deeper. Question was, were the team about to let me pen test a multimillion-dollar racing car?

I still had the access to the build code, which included the password files. The passwords were hashed, so I asked for permission to attempt to crack the root hash using John the Ripper. The password was cracked within about 25 minutes, it was 'xtpassword'. Ten lowercase letters, the dividing line between anyone with engineering network access, and the ability to login to a racing car. I guess I shouldn't have been surprised; after all, nuclear power plant control systems had been discovered with security just as lax.

I concocted a new scenario. Rather than tampering with the operating system code and pushing that to the car ahead of time, could someone simply be logging in to the operating system during the race and somehow be impacting performance? Normally, when faced with a suspected intrusion scenario, the first things you look at are logs. Given that the checksums matched on both the build from the car, and the version from the code repository, I could be sure that there were no log files or other temporary data stored in the build. Keith confirmed that the only place temporary data was stored on the car during operation was a volatile ram disk. When the car was turned off, the data was lost; everything else was on a read-only file system, a bit like launching an operating system from a live CD. If someone was connecting to the car, it wasn't going to hold the vital evidence that proved that to be the case. I'd need to locate the system that was being used to as the gateway to the car. I also needed to be one hundred percent sure that the SSH daemon on the operating system would be running under normal circumstances.

.

Fortunately, the team had an emulator, which meant the car did not need to be the target of engagement for my pen testing activities. I worked late, and confirmed that SSH was a service presented to the engineering network while the car was operational. This was a major breakthrough, but I was still a long way off from proving anything. I left the factory for the night, calling Dave and explaining where I was at with the investigation. I told him that the next few hours would be pivotal in confirming my suspicions, and that we might need to do some device seizures the next day. He promised to assist as best he could, but reiterated that time, and budget was running short.

Racing for Answers: Chapter Four

I was probably the first person at the factory the next morning, as the night shift filed out; I headed in, with several sterile disks and my write blocker kit. I synced up with Dave, and requested that the IT manager join us. I was going to need his help in tracking down what, if anything may have accessed the car, and ultimately if there was evidence of an intrusion, who was responsible.

I'd noticed during my code review, that the car's IP addresses were hard coded static addresses. Keith Hartwell had also confirmed yesterday that each car had a unique static IP. What I needed, were internal network logs that showed traffic heading to the cars source IP. I was frustrated, but not surprised to find that no such logs existed for internal connections. This is a fairly common for traffic on the same network segment. However, there was a glimmer of hope.

"The cars connect back via VPN, right? So surely there is a VPN endpoint or something that they are hitting that may have some logs on it?" I asked longingly to the IT manager. He wasn't sure about the logs, but he confirmed the presence of the VPN router and was able to login to it. At the console, he typed 'show log'. There were logs in the local log buffer showing historic traffic originating from the cars. Three different destination IP addresses that the cars were talking to were present, and we performed a furious discovery exercise to find out what they were. They were all telemetry servers, and the traffic was considered 'legit'.

My next idea was to ask the IT manager to perform a packet capture during the next race. My thought was that if someone were connecting to the cars, they would only be doing this during times the car was on. I showed him a couple of commands to isolate traffic to and from the cars, and dump them to a file called 'capture.cap'. My demonstration consisted of me running the command for about 60 seconds and then showing him how to copy that capture file from the VPN router back to his machine. In doing so, I created an actual packet capture file called 'capture.cap'. I was expecting it to be an empty file. It wasn't, some traffic had been captured during the course of my sixty-second demonstration.

"Weird…" I thought to myself, and opened the capture file in Wireshark.

An ICMP packet was in the capture. The destination IP was the car; the source was an IP address unknown to me.

"Would anyone be trying to ping the car right now?" I asked the IT manager. He didn't know, so suggested that we get Keith Hartwell in the room. Keith came up to Dave's office, and reviewed what I'd captured.

"Mmmm.. there is absolutely no reason that I know of for a machine to be sending out ping packets to a car. Unless someone has invented a life check script or something like that. What is the name of the machine sending the ping?" Keith said sheepishly.

Meanwhile, the IT manager had a machine name that was behind the source IP. It was a workstation; he was in the process of working out whose workstation. While this was going on, I'd created capture2.cap, which at this point had about ten minutes of data in it. There were twenty packets captured, each one an ICMP echo request packet, sent to both cars IP addresses at sixty-second intervals.

The IT manager came up with the name of the owner of the machine, it was the software engineer I'd met several days earlier. Why was his machine pinging the cars every minute, even during a time window when he, as a member of the team would know that they were off in the back of a transporter? Everyone in the room was in agreement that something was not quite right. We needed to examine that machine.

Dave wanted to make sure we went about this the right way, and by right way, he means right way as far as the HR department was concerned. He asked me if we should consider the engineer a suspect. I told him absolutely, he had the means and opportunity; all we needed to find was a motive and we'd have probable cause.

Still searching for specific examples of why this machine would be trying to ping the cars, Keith cautioned that there may still be an innocent reason behind the activity, and that this engineer had been with the team for an extremely long time, and as far as he was concerned was of solid character.

Dave had asked the head of HR to join us in his ever-crowding office. We agreed a two-pronged approach. She and Dave would ask the engineer to join them in Dave's office for a chat, while myself, Keith and the IT manager would perform a live acquisition of the machine. We waited outside of the software engineering office for the all clear to go in. Approaching the empty desk, I removed my camera and started to photograph the desk and surroundings. This could be a crime scene, and photos of how things were found are an extremely important record from both an investigation and legal perspective. Dave and the HR manager planned to brief the engineer on what was happening, so I'd asked Dave to ensure that at no point was the engineer in possession of a mobile device. I didn't want him triggering something remotely to hide evidence.

We were now performing the live acquisition to the sterile media. I'd agreed with the group that we'd take two live images, then power off the machine and secure it offsite. There were also three USB sticks on the desk, these were also seized and a separate image was taken of each via my USB write blocker.

Once all the images were complete, I'd bagged and tagged everything and prepared to head back to the lab. Dave caught me.

"This guy, he's absolutely distraught… he swears that there is no reason that his machine should be pinging the cars, and is adamant that he hasn't done anything wrong. I'm inclined to believe him at the moment." I told Dave that if the engineer were innocent, we'd find evidence to support that.

"I understand, I've dealt with cases where someone has been trying to frame a colleague before. I will keep that in mind." I tried to reassure him. The engineer had been suspended from work on full pay while the investigation was on going.

I raced back to the lab, no pun intended. I began to process the first live image, while using software to boot into the second one. This special tool allowed me to interact with a live copy of a system without changing the contents of the image. Pretty impressive, and there is nothing better than being able to show a courtroom exactly what you are taking about when working with a disk image.

The first thing I noticed with this machine was the lack of antivirus software. As a security guy, it's kind of a subconscious thing for me to check when working with a machine. That is especially true when the machine belongs to a software developer. Developers have a habit of turning off antivirus to improve performance when it comes to compile time. After a quick, non-scientific browse around the machine, I found nothing else that looked out of place.

Next I reviewed volatile data I'd captured from the machine using Forensic Toolkit, at this point I still had my first image processing, so believed this to be a good use of this time. The volatile data snapshot I'd taken included DLL hooks and open network connection data. I reviewed the open network connection data. Several open network connections to Google, Microsoft and Apple were present, as was extremely common. This is usually indicative of software updates being downloaded from those respective sources. Then I noticed a connection that made my mouth drop. It was a reverse connection to an IP I knew extremely well. The IP address belonging to the satellite broadband connection, that Aaron Shelley's account had logged in from during the Spanish test. The IP address that was not used by XT. What had this connection open, and why?

The Forensic Toolkit listed the process that had the open socket. It was a process that I didn't recognise, so did some online searching. I found a reference to the process name, on a website about the Zeus Trojan horse.

This machine was infected, and its command and control server belonged on the network of a rival team! Could that really be true? There were still a lot of questions to be answered before that could be officially declared. Cyber warfare between two racing teams? That would be pretty extreme, but given the amount of money involved in the sport, the sport was more like a business than anything else, and there have been plenty of examples of business rivals engaging in cyber espionage.

I needed to work out a couple of things. Did that IP really belong to another team? How did the malware get on the machine? Did malware on this machine impact the car in any way, and if so, how?

I knew of at least one rival team that used the satellite broadband provider who owned that IP address thanks to my earlier research, so I could be sure that they were a customer. I just needed to link them to the IP.

Now, if I rang up the broadband provider and asked which customer was behind a given IP, I probably wouldn't get an answer. So, I did the next best thing. I found the name of an executive at the rival team, and rang the broadband provider support hotline. I told them I needed to know my networks external IP address to allow a third-party cloud service to set me up with access to their product, and that it was urgent. Sure enough, after a few tense minutes on hold, the answer came back. They gave me the IP address that perfectly matched the one I'd seen in the access log, and in the volatile data from the engineer's machine. Things just got very interesting.

While all this had been going on, my image had finished processing. The Forensic Toolkit had a malware analysis feature turned on, which confirmed the presence of Zeus, as well as a couple of other files that were labelled as 'potentially malicious'. Those potentially malicious files contained elements found in other malware, and after a quick bit of research, I found that they were malware building blocks from a do it yourself malware toolkit that had been leaked online earlier in the year. Then it hit me. Someone had compromised this machine, installed the Zeus Trojan, and then used it to push a custom piece of malware that had been designed to specifically attack the racing cars. I extracted the DIY'ed malware files and transferred them to my malware sandbox environment.

Executing the custom malware and watching for network traffic, I started to see ICMP packets addressed to the cars trying to leave the sandbox machine. Incredible, I thought to myself. The ICMP packets are likely a life check for some further action. I wanted to know what that action was, so I decided on another experiment.

I spun up a Kippo SSH honeypot in the sandbox environment. I set the root password to 'xtpassword' and configured the IP address to match one of those found on a car. Executing the malware, I saw that once it had received the ping response from the Kippo VM, it logged in using the root username and password and began executing a series of commands.

I needed to know exactly what those commands did, so I phoned Keith Hartwell. Through my description of each command, he said in a terrified tone, that he believed the malware was re-enabling the P2CA module, which would allow for pit to car adjustments. I executed the other malware files. One appeared to undo that change, while another appeared to send a series of parameters to a configuration file. Keith confirmed that those parameters would alter the gear ratios and engine settings, slowing the car down.

I called Dave Simmonds to explain what I'd found. His excitement was overshadowed only by his fury. He wanted to know exactly how the malware had gotten onto the machine. I assured him that we'd find out.

That part of the investigation would take me back to the first place I'd seen that IP address, the engineering network access logs. The logs had tied Aaron Shelley's account to the other teams IP. I thought it unlikely that Shelley had been involved, so I wanted to prove beyond any reasonable doubt that this was the case. I looked at emails that Shelley had received and found one that caught my attention. The subject line of the mail followed the pattern of messages I'd seen sent out by the XT IT team, but unlike others, the subject was entirely in lower case. Normally it seemed the IT team formatted their subject lines in title case.

I examined the 'off looking' mail, and before long I could tell it was a phishing message. The body of the email requested that all employees should login to a new portal to claim special offers for XT staff. An attempt to review the link was fruitless because it was now dead, but I strongly suspected that it was likely that Shelley had fallen victim to the scam and unknowingly handed over his password. That password would then have subsequently been used to access the XT engineering network.

But how do you go from having remote access to the network, to installing Zeus on the exact machine that held the operating system code for the cars? There were still a few gaps to fill in.

I decided to make myself a coffee. While it was brewing, I browsed the website of the rival team. There were pages with bios of the management team and the drivers. A name jumped out at me. Sergjei Utkin, he was listed as a test driver for the rival team. Reading his bio, I could see that he'd joined after being released by XT.

Compared to a racing driver, the life of a test driver is pretty bland. They rarely get to drive the cars, and spend most of their time putting in hours in a simulator. The salary paled in comparison. Was Utkin trying to seek revenge against his former employer? Did he have the knowledge and technical ability to phish Aaron Shelley, or did he have help? Perhaps from his buddy on the inside? Would a software engineer knowingly install Zeus and custom malware on their machine?

I decided to review the email conversations between Utkin and the engineer that I'd already studied earlier in the investigation. At the time, nothing had jumped out at me, but given the new information I had, there was absolutely no reason not to review them again. One of those messages contained a link, and a reference to Uktin's brother.

"You should check out my brother's website, he collects cars" Utkin had said.

I followed the link, and it looked like a completely normal, cheesy, 'geocities' era web page. The page had several sections that seemed to be dedicated to the creator's hobbies. He did have a car collection, and was also interested in web site development and coding. The creator went by the name of Vadim Utkin, so this did appear to be another member of the Utkin clan. I clicked onto the car section. Just then, my browser popped up with a Noscript warning. Noscript was a plugin that I used to block JavaScript from executing on my machine without my permission. Just another paranoid security guy tool, although one I recommended to everyone.

The name of the script that was trying to execute was 'beefhook.js'. I'd knew right away that this code was attempting to 'hook' my browser with a tool known as the Browser Exploitation Framework, or 'beef' for short. Beef was a tool that attackers could leverage to perform a client-side attack. An attack against a web-browsing client accessing a malicious site.

One of the features of Beef is the ability to pull information from the victim machine once it was hooked, information such as the IP address and hostname. This was my eureka moment, for the first time during the investigation all the pieces fell together.

Utkin, upset at his being cut from the driver development program had teamed up with his brother to create a piece of malware that could sabotage XT Racing cars. He knew from his time in the driver development program, the name of an engineer, his friend, whose machine had code for the on-board operating system. Utkin's brother had set up a malicious website that would perform a client side attack against the engineer's machine; this was probably designed to push the Zeus Trojan. For some reason, that didn't work as they expected. They may have got some information from the machine, such as hostname or internal IP, but for whatever reason couldn't push Zeus so they needed another way in to the network.

They targeted a non-IT savvy employee, Aaron Shelley, a racing driver, in a second phishing attack. Utkin would have known that Shelley had an account due to being a member of the driver development program. This worked, and they were able to get a valid set of credentials and gain remote access to the network. From there, they installed Zeus on the engineer's machine.

Utkin's brother would have used his remote access to the machine to access the operating system code, and developed the custom malware. He staged his payload locally and trained his brother Sergjei on deploying the malware during the races, to slow the cars. Unfortunately, Sergjei operated the command and control server for Zeus from the garage of the rival team, using their broadband connection. This was the only slip up in a highly-sophisticated attack; the broadband IP address had been the key component in tying everything together.

I sat back in my chair, took a deep breath and called Dave, where I ran through my findings.

Racing for Answers: Epilogue

In the days that followed, XT Racing handed all of the evidence over to the sport's governing body. The governing body approached the rival team with an ultimatum; allow us access to your network to perform an internal investigation, or face legal action. They opted for the internal investigation. I was not asked to be a part of this investigation, but I was kept in the loop by XT. They found the Zeus command and control server on a laptop used by Utkin while he was in the garage.

The team claimed they had no knowledge of Utkin's activities, and he was fired. The governing body didn't care, and ordered that the team not receive any points during that year's championship, which also meant they did not get a single cent in prize money. The surrounding bad press also drove away team sponsors.

XT Racing thanked me for my efforts and rewarded me with VIP treatment at the next race, where I sat in an executive box, sipping a Mimosa, being a tosspot. A happy tosspot, as I watched my new friends at XT win their first race of the season.

Crossbow

Crossbow: Chapter One

Phones always seem to ring at the most inconvenient times. Today was no exception, just as I was beginning a software upgrade in the lab; the little bugger lit up and started to chime away. However, one must always remember, if the phone doesn't ring, there will be no money to pay the phone bill.

When I say lit up, I literally mean lit up. As a joke gift several years earlier, one of my colleagues decided the lab phone wasn't enough of a 'bat phone', so she bought me one to hang off of our incident response hotline. As a result, a call to this number automatically triggered a combination of lights and sound that would amuse even the most upset and uninterested infant, as it did me, which should tell you a lot about my sense of humour.

I picked up the phone, and introduced myself to the caller. The caller reciprocated.

"My name is Richard Groves, I co-own a company called AviVector Technologies, and I think I need your help."

After a discussion with Richard of around twenty minutes, three key points stuck out in my mind. The first was that Richard was an extremely smart guy, much smarter than myself. He was a pilot, software developer and had gone on to combine these two skills with the formation of a highly successful company, AviVector. He owned fifty percent of this company. The other half was broken up between two brothers. They were investors whom Richard had met while working on a project in South Africa five years earlier.

The second point was that Richard was in need of fast help. He'd explained how his company was moving into the world of commercial drones. These were pilotless aircraft that would be used principally for surveillance, photography and mapping. He'd explained how this was a massive growth area. Several companies were moving into the space and therefore, his company needed an edge. His company's edge, were the algorithms embedded within the drone software.

So, for Richard and his company, the worst possible scenario for him would be if someone had their hands on these algorithms, they were intellectual property of immeasurable value.

Unfortunately, the reason Richard called was because he believed that the worst-case scenario had occurred, although he hadn't gone into too much detail over the phone. That would have to wait until we were face to face in the morning.

The final point that resonated in my head after my conversation with Richard was that he and his company seemed incredibly security aware. Their facility had been awarded List X status three years prior, which gave them the right to work on highly sensitive government projects by virtue of meeting several stringent security requirements. They even had an information security manager.

So, with that in mind, I would have thought their prized algorithms would be difficult to steal. Of course, with any information security management system, there are exceptions and flaws. What looks great on paper and screen doesn't always play out that way in real life. But still, I imagined interesting times ahead with this case.

Having cancelled my pending software update, I began consulting the Internet for more information on AviVector and made plans on how best to proceed.

I had arranged to head out to my newly acquired client in the morning, their facility was located in the Cotswolds, on the site of an old Royal Air Force base. As you may expect, I'd discovered the address via their public website.

In the industry, we call information posted online and made public, 'open source information'. In my time, I've discovered that not all clues, or clues to other clues are hidden deep within a case, but can be found in plain sight in open source locations. With half of the day still to go, and no further information from the inside forthcoming until at least the following morning, I planned on spending the afternoon learning all I could about AviVector from Mr. Google and friends.

Incorporation documents, patents, press releases, job openings, and news stories were all printed off and arranged on my desk. I am aware, of course, that this is no longer acceptable, and that I shouldn't be printing anything anymore, but for some reason I find things a million times easier to note when working with a piece of paper and a highlighter. So, sorry folks, even in the hi-tech world I've found myself working in, occasionally the low-tech approach wins out.

From the incorporation documents, I could see the names of the three founders. Alongside Richard, were David and Eric Bester. These were the two brothers that Richard had mentioned earlier.

The Bester brothers were promptly Googled, and mentioned in several news stories where they'd been promoting their various interests. David Bester had a small investment company website, where it appeared he was involved in mostly software and technology related investments. Eric was the older one, David about five years younger. Now in their late thirties, they both appeared to be married, and Eric had two kids. The latter information was gathered from Facebook, which, if you don't apply appropriate privacy controls is still a source of open source information if you ask me.

Aside from some sloppy social media usage, little else of note could be found on David and Eric. Richard himself had such a common name, that it was hard to determine if he even had a social media account of any kind. Even if he did, from our brief chat, I imagined that it'd be locked down tight. Richard had left an impression of a sensible chap as well as a smart chap, which are two very different personality traits. Having both is an incredibly difficult thing to achieve in my book.

The company appeared to employ somewhere in the region of 50 people, and job openings suggested a trend towards picking up recent computer science graduates.

A press release announced a contract to supply software for Air Traffic Control equipment in Hong Kong and Mainland China. AviVector were the principle vendor on the project, working with a local subcontractor who would provide localisation services.

Although there were a couple more press releases relating to the aviation software side of the business, I couldn't find anything of relevance to the drone related ventures.

What about the famed information security manager, mentioned earlier by Richard? It's always interesting when a CEO or other senior manager calls me, and not the information security managers themselves. It usually means that they know that the information security manager may have royally messed something up, is too proud to ask for help on their own, or may not be trusted for whatever reason to handle the incident by their senior management. It would be a question for Richard to answer, this much was for sure.

It was at this point that the lights and sound of the phone once again interrupted my open source intelligence gathering. My immediate concern was that I had another case that I'd have to juggle with this one. My concerns were unfounded.

"Hi Parker, it's Richard from AviVector again…" came the muted voice down the wire.

"Everything okay?" I enquired.

"Not really, things have actually escalated somewhat significantly, and I hate to ask, but any chance you can come to our offices right now?"

I looked at the clock and knew that in just a few hours my beloved Aston Villa were due to take on Chelsea in a must win cup game which was due to be presented on a big screen telly at my local pub. This made me hesitant to commit, it was late in the afternoon and I had plans. Plans involving friends, sports and drinking. However, I'm a sucker for a case like this, or any case for that matter. I knew deep down Villa would lose anyway. With no further ado, I jumped in my car and told my wife I'd be home late, for probably the millionth time in our history.

On the drive over, I pondered what had happened to increase the urgency of the situation. Surely someone either had the algorithms or they didn't? Perhaps the incident was still ongoing and data was being exfiltrated? I'd find out soon enough.

Crossbow: Chapter Two

I headed into the business park located on the old RAF base. The main entrance took me a down a long spinal road, punctuated by roundabouts every two hundred yards or so. I couldn't help but notice that the number of headlights heading toward me out of the park was significantly greater than the number of red brake lights in front of me heading in. Still, I managed to find myself stuck behind a Ford Sierra whose exhaust system had seen better days, the choking smoke making it appear like I was heading into the abyss through a thick fog. The now sub-zero temperatures amplifying the effect.

After a wrong turn and a trip back to the spinal road, I located AviVector's building. It looked like a fortress compared to some of the other buildings in the park. There was a single gated entrance to a car park with about 30 spaces in it, and a razor wire fence. I introduced myself to the well bundled up security guard, and showed him my ID. Richard had apparently put me on the visitor list, so no problem there. The guard asked me if I had any electronic equipment with me. I said yes, a phone and laptop. Of course, I also had a bag full of write blockers and sterile media, but one usually wants to keep the presence of such equipment on the down-low.

"The laptop and phone can only be taken in rooms designated as Red Rooms", said the guard. "Do not attempt to take them into any Green Rooms."

"Ok, got it, seems easy to remember, thanks…" I nodded and smiled towards him. I'm not really sure if I was expecting a smile back, but in any case, I never got one.

I parked the car and walked into the building, the reception desk was empty given the time of day, so I pressed the buzzer on the desk and waited for someone to emerge from the office area.

"Parker?" came a voice out of nowhere. I turned around to see a man who looked like he was having a bad day, so I assumed that this must be Richard.

"Hi, Richard, nice to meet you." We shook hands and Richard beckoned me through a door that ultimately led to his office. I was slightly in awe of pictures of aircraft flight decks kitted out with the latest equipment, which one would imagine AviVector had some part in creating. Shelves behind Richard's desk were full of scale models of planes, helicopters and spacecraft.

Richard sat me down at his desk, and spun around his large computer monitor to face me.

"This is what I've received today, the first one is on the left, and the second one is one the right."

Richard was referring to two side-by-side emails, which filled his screen. As I started to read the first email, Richard started to speak.

"My initial ask of you was to tell me if you thought the first email was real, but I think the second email answers that question. So, my next question is what the hell do I do about this??"

"Okay, just a sec..." I was trying to get my head around the contents of the mail.

The emails were essentially ransom notes, written in broken English. The first one provided an introduction to the 'kidnappers'.

"We are group of Turkish hackers, the Bayrampaşa Boys, your organisation work for us now." The ominous opening line read. "We have all the source code for your Crossbow…"

"I assume that Crossbow is the name of your drone software program?" I asked Richard.

"Correct, it's a collection of software and algorithms that control every function of the drone, they allow it to manage its own flight in the event it loses contact with a ground station. It is highly sensitive, and is our most valuable intellectual property", he replied. I returned to the email.

"In 48 hours, we will start to publish the Crossbow code, 20% at a time via Pastebin." Pastebin is a public clipboard, and a preferred service used by hackers to publically disclose their breaches.

"We will not publish if you complete the transfer of $2.5 million US, via a Bitcoin exchange." The message continued.

"We are reasonable people, and will ask only for $250,000 in Bitcoin within the first 48 hours. After that you have to complete 9 more $250,000 instalments every 72 hours. Please confirm you have read this message within 8 hours, otherwise we will be forced to act sooner."

"Mmm… and I thought my credit card company were unreasonable." I said, half-jokingly to try and help return some the colour to Richard's rapidly paling skin. It didn't work.

"At first, this scared me." Richard said. "No one should know the name of the project outside of the folks working on the software. Then, I got the second email, and that almost made me collapse with fear." I began to scan the second email.

"We receive no response from you. In case you think we are playing a game, see below…" Directly underneath this line was a block of code.

"I assume that this is actually part of your source code?" I asked.

Richard nodded.

"Have you responded at all to these messages yet?"

"No I haven't, not yet, I haven't even discussed them with my partners. The second email was the escalation I mentioned earlier. I need your help."

I began to ponder Richard's predicament. Personally, I had never heard of the Bayrampaşa Boys, but clearly whoever was on the other end of these messages had some of the code, and weren't afraid to show it. First thing we needed to do was establish the facts around who had access to that code. Had it really been stolen, or was this an insider trying to pull a fast one. Secondly, I needed to know if this supposed hacker group was real, and if they had set any precedents. In the meantime, I thought it best that Richard respond and appear cooperative.

"Respond to the mail, and say you understand the agreement, and are working on the first deposit. That costs you nothing, and can only serve to buy you time." I instructed Richard.

"Okay. Got it, will do that now. These bastards…"

"Incidentally, is that ransom something AviVector could absorb if necessary?" I asked.

Richard looked at me, and sighed.

"Perhaps, we would need to make some transactions, and probably lose a couple of staff to make it happen, and it would hurt us, but on balance, having the code leaked would hurt us more. We'd lose our edge in the drone wars, and probably our List X status. No one would touch us again. All the work, gone in an instant."

His sentiment summed up the impact of a data breach perfectly. I wanted to help him.

"Let's start by talking about how exactly your code is stored, and who has access to it." I said, pen and notepad eagerly at the ready to start capturing information.

"Well, before we do that, I really have to go and speak to Dave and Eric, to keep them in the loop about what is going on here… I'll be right back." Richard picked up his phone and went through a back door into another office, which was completely empty by now.

While Richard was out, I noticed that we were in one of the aforementioned Red Rooms, so laptops and equipment were fine to be used. I wanted to get online to start researching the Bayrampaşa Boys. AviVector had a guest Wi-Fi network, however I also carried a cellular dongle to avoid having to use potentially compromised networks.

Bayrampaşa, according to Mr. Google, was a working-class suburb of Istanbul. Immediately, something didn't seem right. Hacker groups tend to want to be anonymous, and in order to take advantage of the shroud provided by the Internet, one doesn't tend to go around naming your group after a real location, not this specifically anyway.

There was also no mention of this hacker group online, anywhere. No mention of database dumps, DDoS ransoms, stolen credentials or defaced web pages attributable to said group. It seemed to me that either someone was bluffing, or new to this particular game.

Richard re-entered the room, and sat down.

"Well… Eric is upset and is freaking out, says to do whatever we need to do to deal with this. Dave is being slightly less panicky, and he says he will work on a plan to pay the fee if we need to get it paid", he said. "Dave is always the one you can rely on to keep his head in a crisis."

I explained to Richard that I'd found nothing on the Bayrampaşa Boys, and explained my suspicions around the fact that a real hacker group would not likely name itself after a physical location.

"Richard, at the moment, I think we have to consider the possibility that an insider is responsible for this. Would you support investigating that theory?"

"As much as it pains me to do so, I consider everyone here to be a friend, I think that it is only sensible course of action."

I could tell that Richard was genuinely upset at the thought of someone inside the company he'd built trying to extort him, but I was glad that he was sensible enough to realise that it was a valid possibility.

"The only issue I have with the idea of it being an insider, is that I am the only person with the required access to all of the Crossbow code. We operate a very tight source code control scheme here. Everything is modular. No single developer has access to the entire code repository."

"What about someone who isn't a developer? Systems engineer, or administrator perhaps?" I suggested.

"We've got that covered too, the modular code repositories are encrypted, so although an admin has access to the machine, they cannot have access to the encrypted code."

"Who manages the keys?"

"I do", said Richard.

"Does anyone else have access to your credentials?"

"That's impossible, we use tri-factor authentication on our Crossbow network." Richard showed me a smartcard, and an application on his phone that generated a one-time password. These two pieces of information, plus a 15-character static password were required to gain access to the AviVector Crossbow network.

"And before you ask, the network where the code is written and stored is air-gapped from the Internet."

It was clear to me that this was a company that took security extremely seriously, not just on paper, but in practice too. So how then, could they find themselves in this situation?

"These controls are impressive Richard, you really seem to be doing everything you can here."

Recapping what we'd just discussed, I asked Richard to confirm my understanding that his account was the only account with access to all of the code, the code was stored on an air-gapped system, and the only way to access his account was using a plethora of authentication devices.

"I read on your website you have an Information Security Manager, is that true?" I enquired.

"Oh yes, Paul Stern, he is extremely talented, and helped us set up all of the controls we've just discussed."

"Sorry to be so blunt, but can I ask why he isn't here right now, given that this is a pretty serious security incident?"

"Oh yes, Paul is taking a much-needed holiday. He has worked here for two years, and this is the first time he has been able to take a break. If I call him, he'll jump on a plane and get back here. He needs this holiday; I don't want him to worry about this. We can deal with it on our own."

"I see, well given that Paul helped set up the security program here could he be respon…" I couldn't finish my sentence before Richard interrupted.

"Oh, honestly Parker I don't think…
I mean, I'd be extremely surprised, if he
was involved in this. Throughout the
years, he has been very transparent about
not wanting to become a 'superuser' with
all the access in the world. He is
extremely sensitive to that kind of
thing."

"Ok, understood."

Having thought about it some more,
it didn't make much sense to me for an
information security manager to want to
extort his own company by means of staging
a fake breach, unless they were struggling
to get support for their program, which
clearly wasn't an issue here. I tabled
that theory for now.

I returned to my notes, and started
to run theories in my head.

"Ok, so given that each developer
only has modular access to code. Can we
find out which developer wrote the code
snippet contained in the email from the
supposed hackers?"

"Yes, certainly." Richard said as he
stood up. He led me to the door.

"We'll need to go and access the
code on one of the Crossbow lab machines.
You'll have to leave your phone and laptop
here I'm afraid."

We walked together down the
corridor, which turned out to be 'L'
shaped. As we turned the corner, I was
surprised to see another security guard,
this time on the internal door; he had a
hand-held metal detector.

"Hello Richard, any mobile devices, USB drives?" he said as he ran the detector over him. This was very impressive from a security point of view; a guard was checking one of the owners of the company, as if he were anyone else, just as it should be.

"Nah. I knew you were on today, so I didn't want to cause you any hassle, I know how grumpy you can get." Richard joked with the guard.

"How about you sir?" The guard turned his attention to me.

"Nothing to declare!" I responded. It really did feel like I was at the airport.

"Okay, you're good, go ahead." The guard buzzed us both into the room.

As we entered the room, lights automatically switched on. The room was divided into two halves; to one side it seemed to resemble a traditional electrical engineering lab, filled with ammeters and probes. On the other, there was a cluster of computers. I noticed half a dozen surveillance cameras dotted throughout the room.

The air was dry, and a chorus of server and networking gear fans provided the background noise. It was a very clean space.

Richard had begun the login procedure on one of the computers.

"So, Richard, you mentioned earlier that these machines are on an air-gapped network?"

"Correct, this whole room is isolated from the rest of the company." He made a few keystrokes, and made a note on a pad of paper.

"So, the block of code we saw earlier was written by a developer named Joe Jowett." I wrote the name down.

"What can you tell me about Joe?" I asked.

"Well, he has been with us for probably about two years, he came to us straight from university, although I forget which one. Pleasant enough chap."

"Has he ever shown signs of being disgruntled, or unhappy here?"

"No, I don't think so, every time I've spoken to him about his job he seems to be grateful to have been given it."

"Great, thanks, so aside from your own account and Joe's account, there is no one else who could possibly have had access to this block of code?"

"No, I can guarantee that."

At this point in the investigation, we had the name of a possible suspect; an insider with the means to steal the only part of the code we knew for sure had been stolen. The next step was trying to determine motive. I conversed with Richard on the way back to his office.

"When you say, Joe had the means to steal the code, how do you think he stole it?" Richard enquired. "I mean, you've seen all the security in place in there."

"Well, he might not have 'stolen' it per se." I replied.

"How do you mean?"

"Well, think of where the code came from, the code came from the brain of an organism named Joe. He transferred it to your computer via the keyboard. He could very easily go to his home computer, or even another computer in this very office and use a keyboard to transfer it into there." In my experience, 'techies' often overlook human factors. Richard realised he'd just done that and looked slightly embarrassed.

"Wouldn't life be simple if we could just re-image the minds of developers at the end of every day, just as we do our laptops when they come back from trips outside of the office!" Richard joked.

"You sir, have been watching too much 'Men in Black!'"

Crossbow: Chapter Three

We'd been back in Richards's office for only a handful of minutes when he told me he'd received a new email from the group. It was an acknowledgement of the email Richard had sent earlier, and also encouraged him to be mindful of the first deadline. Then towards the end of the email there was a line that made Richard turn almost fully transparent. The sender reiterated that they weren't bluffing, and to add weight to that point they'd attached an additional code block.

"This is a part of one of the core algorithms for unassisted navigation of the drone. This is really bad Parker!" Richard had his head in his hands.

"Richard, did Joe Jowett write this code?" I knew that if he did, he'd almost certainly be the source of the leak, one way or another. If he didn't, Joe may very well be off the hook for this one. Richard shook his head.

"I know for a fact he didn't."

"How so?"

"Because I wrote this code!"

By now Richard looked devastated. If this was code he'd handcrafted, his account was the only one that had access to it. Had someone been able to compromise his account, and with the authentication layers, how was this even possible?

The phone rang, Richard said it was David Bester, and he'd step out to take the call. I quickly asked for permission to view the email headers from the latest message. The emails were the only piece of evidence we had with the kidnapper's electronic fingerprints. I figured I should rule out any chance there could be evidence of true source contained in the headers. Of course, I could locate the sending server's IP address from the headers, but most of the time that would just be some random compromised box hosted by a less than reputable hosting service.

Sure enough, that was the case today. A French server hosting a fashion website and about seventy others, with an open SMTP relay, doing their part to keep the global spam levels high.

"Well, whoever is doing this knows how to use an open SMTP relay." I said to Richard as he returned from his call.

"Parker, David has figured out how we can pay the ransom if needed. He said we'll give it a couple of hours and if we have to start paying we will. He doesn't want this to get out there." I could tell Richard was slightly anxious about that decision.

"Also, I didn't tell him that this contained some of my code. Not looking forward to that discussion."

"Well Richard clearly you didn't give the code away on purpose. I think someone stole it using your account. We just need to find out how." I paused for a second. "Given that this environment has such high security, and you are so dedicated, I have to ask, did you put this code together or work on it outside of the environment?"

Richard smiled and began to respond.

"I have to thank you for wording that question so favourably, however, as my wife will be able to confirm, I don't work on code at home. I stay in the office for extremely long hours and work on it here. I sit at the same machine in the lab for hours."

I stood up.

"Let's go and look at that machine then!"

Richard nodded.

I went to grab my bag containing my write blocking equipment and laptop on the way out of his office.

"Whoa. You can't take any of that stuff into the lab, not even for this."

"Richard, if we are looking at a machine that potentially contains evidence of an exfiltration from your company, then we are going to have to use this equipment, it's the only way we can preserve the state of the machine." Richard looked conflicted.

"Worst case scenario, this gets out and the entire company knows that your account was used to leak the code, and there is no evidence in place to suggest that you didn't do it on purpose. This is as much for your own protection, as it is the company's."

"Okay, I understand that. I don't really understand why anyone would feel the need to set me up though."

We headed to the lab room once again, this time we had to explain to the guard why we were taking it some strange looking equipment, including an outside laptop. He was unsure, but given that Richard was the boss, he wasn't really in a position to prevent him from entering his own room. We entered and sat down at Richard's desktop machine, it was already powered down.

My intent was to forensically image the machine's hard drive and run that image as a read-only virtual machine on my laptop using some special software I had for this task. This way I would have the benefits of being able to explore the machine without touching the original. Fortunately, the machine itself had low disk usage. According to Richard it would just contain the operating system and a software development environment. Most of the actual code was stored, encrypted, on a server locked in the rack. The desktop machines connected to the server via mapped network drives. The server would have been a trickier proposition to image so quickly, so I wanted to avoid doing that unless there was absolutely nothing of value on the desktop machine.

The imaging process completed, so I ran the virtual machine directly from the acquired image. Richard helped me work through some of the authentication prompts, and before I knew it, I was sat on a virtualised version of his desktop machine, looking at the same things he would be if he was about to start a day, or night, of hard-core coding.

The machine was pretty unspectacular as expected, and since it wasn't able to connect to the Internet, free of all the associated Internet fodder, like temporary files, plugins and toolbars.

As I was browsing around the control panel to see how the machine was set up, I noticed the on-board software firewall was enabled, and had a custom policy. Even though this machine was on a network that had no Internet access, there was still a strict firewall policy in place. It could only talk to the code server, and only an administrator could change that policy. These guys really had everything locked down to the max.

I reviewed event logs. Of primary interest to me would be whether or not that firewall policy had been changed at any time.

It didn't look like it had, and I looked for gaps in the logs that might indicate that they'd been tampered with. Nothing. There were the same event types and volumes at around the same times each day. It was clean.

One thing I'd noticed on the original physical machine was that it had a DVD drive, which was an off-white colour, while the rest of the machine case was black. I asked Richard about it.

"These machines originally had DVD writers in them. For one of our audits, to be able to work on the more sensitive code, we removed the writers and replaced them with some spare read-only drives that we had. Prevents people burning stuff to CD or DVD and running away with it." Another exfiltration avenue was closed.

I spent a good hour reviewing security logs. I pulled every time over the last month that Richard's account had been used to log on to the machine, and asked him to confirm that he was present on the given dates. Every single time he confirmed that the log on was attributable to him.

I looked at Richard. "I've got nothing so far."

I reviewed everything once again, and in doing so sent my mind down a path that I'd been aware of for perhaps the last couple of hours, but had not wanted to go down.

When I was a kid there was an alleyway that made the journey from school to home about five minutes shorter, but it was dark, and the boys who smoked hung out in it. I'd often go the long way around to avoid hassle. On the occasion that I'd go through that alleyway on my own, I'd have this horrible feeling in the pit of my stomach. I had that same feeling now. I was going to go down that alleyway. However, today that alleyway was suspecting that Richard himself was responsible for this, and I was just a pawn in his wider plan. Question was, how would I approach that?

Richard had seemed incredibly genuine since the moment I'd met him, but as I'd previously noted, he was very smart. Ideally, I'd be able to speak with the other owners, to get their unfiltered opinion on Richard and see if they could shed light on a possible motive, but I didn't have that luxury right now.

I decided to continue on, working with Richard until there were no more avenues left to pursue. Innocent until proven guilty, and all that.

I decided to go back to the time-honoured technique of simplification, to make sure I wasn't letting my now tired head get the better of me.

All breaches have one thing in common; X must talk to Y, when they aren't supposed to talk at all. I like to draw out an X and Y on my notepad and fill in the details. More often than not, this approach opens one's eyes to something that may have been missed.

X in this case is a device, most likely the desktop machine I was examining, that contains the source code which Richard's account has access to. Y is an as yet unidentified party. The roads from X to Y are, as I'd discovered, extremely limited.

I tried to think back to previous breaches, that I'd either worked on, or read about that had involved a highly secure air-gapped system.

The immediate cases I could think of were intelligence leaks, during which the perpetrator, who was an insider, used optical media such as DVD's to steal huge chunks of data. Thanks to the DVD drive chop shop operated by AviVector, that wasn't going to be the path from X to Y here.

Then I remembered reading about malware that had targeted highly secure, air-gapped industrial control systems at nuclear power plants. This malware had been spread using USB memory sticks.

These massive capacity, incredibly small and therefore easy to conceal devices are deadly weapons when it comes to exfiltrating data quickly.

"Richard, do you permit USB storage devices in this lab, and if not, is USB disabled to prevent their use?"

"No, we don't allow them, and the guards are trained to spot them. That said we don't disable USB, because some of the equipment we use in this lab requires the use of USB."

I knew that it was not beyond the realms of possibility that someone could sneak in a USB device, and not be questioned on it. Fortunately, this was a Microsoft Windows machine, and there is one place you go on a Windows machine when you want to get a list of every single USB device ever connected to it - the registry. That was my next stop.

Specifically, there are two registry keys that need to be reviewed in order to determine the USB devices that have ever been attached to a machine. The first, simply gives the name of the device. The second, allows you to see the last time that device was attached.

Upon viewing the first key, I instantly saw the tell-all prefix 'usbstor', which told me that a USB storage device had been connected to this machine in its lifetime. The second key, told me that the last time the device had been connected, two weeks earlier at 3pm system time, which was the same as local time, give or take a couple of minutes.

I then correlated this event with the security logs to find out which account was active on the machine at this time.

Richard had logged in about an hour prior to the USB storage event, and didn't log out until he shut down the machine several hours later. I knew that he had stolen the data. Busted. I made sure to record and encrypt my evidence on the laptop before raising the issue with him.

"Richard, I don't quite know how to put this, but there is evidence on this machine that a USB storage device was connected to it while you were working on it."

"You're kidding me!" Richard looked genuinely shocked. I had to try and figure out if he was shocked that he'd been caught out, or shocked that a USB drive had been connected to the machine. I couldn't tell right away.

"I've never, ever plugged a USB storage device into that machine, never ever. And I always log off rather than lock the machine, so it's not like it was unattended or anything." He said.

"So how can we explain this?" I asked. "I've gotta tell you, it doesn't look great for you right now."

Richard sensed my suspicions were increasing.

"Parker, I promise, this is not my doing. Something bad is at play here, I just don't know what it is."

I got up and inspected the machine once again, there was nothing. Perhaps someone snuck in a USB key logger? Nothing was present, and the machine itself used an older style PS/2 keyboard, so that was unlikely.

"Did this keyboard change recently?" I asked.

"No, not at all, it's been the same one forever, it's my specific keyboard." The keyboard was one of those ergonomic ones that I can't use, but apparently Richard liked, so it's not like he wouldn't have noticed it changing.

"Well, something was plugged into this machine, and as far as I can tell it was a storage device."

Richard pointed at one of the cameras, directly above the desk.

"Let's review the video tape from that time and see if something happened."

We left the lab and headed to an office now occupied by the same security guard I'd met outside earlier in the day.

Richard instructed him to show video from a couple of minutes before the USB storage connection event happened, from the perspective of the camera above the desk in the lab. The three of us sat and watched as the video started to roll.

There was Richard, working at his machine. At about thirty seconds into the video we see a different person walk into the lab, he taps Richard on the back and starts talking to him.

"That's David Bester." Richard said, pointing at the screen.

The conversation went on for a few minutes.

"Ah, I remember this, David had just come in from the airport and wanted to say hi before he went home to sleep. He just flew in from a meeting with one of our partners in Shanghai."

David pulled a box out of his top pocket and gave it to Richard, before heading out of the room.

"What was in the box?" I asked.

"Oh, you'll see in a minute, I get it out. It's this little toy remote control helicopter that our partner gave to us. David gave it to me to give to my son."

The video showed Richard taking the mini helicopter toy and controller out of the box, and after connecting the batteries in the controller and reading the instructions, flying the helicopter up and down.

"I'm a sucker for these kinds of toys." Richard said while we watched the video. "It's kind of embarrassing really. I just knew that once I gave it to my son it would be gone forever, so I just got a bit of fun in while I could."

Then the helicopter landed back on the desk, rather abruptly. Richard was inspecting it.

"Batteries ran out in the helicopter, fortunately, they are rechargeable… oh no way!!" Richard exclaimed.

"It recharges using a USB cable, doesn't it? You plugged it into that machine, didn't you?" I asked, before watching it play out in front of me on the video.

"So, Richard, either your machine thinks that that helicopter is a USB storage device, or that helicopter is a USB storage device!"

"Crap, but it just sat there and recharged, nothing ran on the machine. I didn't copy anything to it for Christ's sake!"

"Well, we need to go get that helicopter!"

"It's at home, fine, let's go."

We stood up and headed out of the security office.

"I just hope my boy is asleep when we get there, he isn't going to be too pleased that we are nicking his helicopter. He's freakishly strong and can hurt me when he's pissed off."

"How old is he?" I asked as we made our way out to our cars.

"Six and a half."

Crossbow: Chapter Four

We arrived at Richard's house, which was a traditional 'commuter belt' four bedroom detached. He introduced me to his wife, and his kids.

His wife offered to make me a cup of tea, and I duly accepted the offer.

Richard explained to his son that he and his friend Parker needed to play with his helicopter, and asked if he would let him do so, the boy agreed, mainly because he was being distracted by whatever garbage was on the television at the time.

The helicopter was promptly fetched and brought to our makeshift lab that had been set up on the dining room table, after the appropriate level of tablecloth had been deployed of course.

I connected it to my USB write blocker, which had an LCD screen that displayed any detected device names and serial numbers when a connection was made. Sure enough, upon connecting the helicopter to the charging cable via the USB write blocker, the storage device was detected. Both Richard and myself were in awe. This toy helicopter came loaded with sixteen gigabytes of storage.

I used my imaging software to acquire the storage device. It was a U3 device, which meant it had the ability to launch applications automatically, almost like an auto running CD. This has some benefits, but in the security community, U3 is somewhat frowned upon for this ability.

The U3 device had two partitions, a CD style partition, and a larger normal storage partition.

Richard leaned in on the laptop screen as files began to appear from the image. The files had been deleted, but were of course still readable.

"Holy crap, that is our code." He looked at me. "How the hell did a toy helicopter steal our code?"

"Any files in this list you don't recognise?" I asked.

Richard looked through the list, and pointed to a particular file. It was a script called runner.bat, which had also been deleted, and then there were a couple of executable files a.exe and b.exe.

I examined runner.bat; a windows batch file with about forty lines, including a couple of loops and functions. There were also comment lines. Save for the fact that they gave me a clue as to the origin of the code, they were of no use to me in deciphering the functions as they were written in Mandarin.

It became clear however, that this code was not designed to fly a toy helicopter. I ran the .exe files through an online service that identifies them based on hash values. One was an FTP client; the other was a self-contained mail server. These executable files were called at various stages by the batch file during its execution.

I drew out a crude flow chart of the batch file execution flow, and used this to explain to Richard what I thought was going on.

"Essentially Richard, this code first identifies all storage locations on whatever machine it is plugged into. Then it looks for any files with common source code extensions, .cpp for example, and then copies them to the USB storage. Next it tries to send the messages over email to a free mail account, and if that fails, an FTP server. If it can't connect to either, it leaves the files where they are, then tries the same process again the next time it is run, which would be the next time it is plugged into a machine, any machine." Richard took over the explanation at this point.

"And if that machine is connected to the Internet, it uploads the previously gathered files and then deletes them from the USB!"

"Correct!" I said.

"Wow, my mind is blown by this. I just never thought about that when I plugged a bloody toy helicopter into a machine to charge the batteries. Crazy. So, what do we do next?"

"Well let's get the low down on who gave David that helicopter."

"He told me he got it from VTSD Global, we work with them on several projects in China." This was the same company that I read about online earlier; they'd worked together on the Air Traffic Control software. "Currently we are working with them on several contracts. In fact, one of the ways David suggests that we pay this 'ransom' is by allowing them to buy out one of the contracts. They've never been able to win a bid without us, but they've been growing rapidly and want the chance to go it alone. My concern with that is we'd undervalue the contract so that they would definitely buy it out, and we'd have to lose some of our people, as well as the cash for completing the contract."

"Are you working with VTSD on the Crossbow project, or were you competing with them on it?"

"No not at all. They wouldn't even know about it." Richard got distracted by his phone beeping. "It's David, he wants to know if he should go ahead and offer VTSD the chance to buy the contract, so we can pay this ransom." We both looked at each other.

"Well, considering it looks like VTSD are now a suspect here, I'd recommend you hold off giving them any money." I said.

"But what if they release our code, I can't shake that fear."

"Oh, we'll get to them long before they think about doing that." I smiled. "That said, all we have is David's word that he got this helicopter from them. We really need to get a more definitive link."

"Tell you what, I'll get David over here." Richard said, tapping at his phone. After a brief pause, the phone beeped. "He's on his way."

While waiting for David, I ran the IP address of the FTP server from the code. It belonged to a Spanish web host, and looked like just another compromised server. The batch file also included what appeared to be a username and password, base64 encoded, for that FTP server.

"Though we shouldn't really do this, as we don't have permission from the server owner… I'd like to suggest logging into that FTP server, and seeing if any of your information still lives there. Any objections?" I asked Richard.

"Oh, yes, let's do that. As far as I'm concerned that is fair game."

I logged in via the command line and saw that the FTP server was empty, at least in the home directory; I was able to jump up a directory level. This spoke to the lack of security on this server, but it did provide some useful evidence.

"Log files Richard! We can see who has been connecting to this server."

I downloaded 'access.log', which seemed to have almost a year's worth of access to the FTP server recorded in it.

I performed a quick open source discovery on VTSD Global and found some external IP addresses. I opened the log on my Linux virtual machine, and grepped for their IP addresses. I was hoping to see a VTSD IP address in the log, because of course, that would complete the chain from X to Y.

Nothing. It wasn't there. I didn't have too much time to dwell on that as David had arrived.

Richard went to greet David. While he was bringing him up to speed with the investigation in another room, I decided to find out Richard's home external IP address, to see if I could find that in the log grep. It was there. There had been a connection two weeks ago, at about 8:30pm.

I pulled the list of every unique IP address that had logged into that server, this was about fifty. I ran them through a script to do hostname lookup and also run a WHOIS record search. WHOIS records identify the organisation that owns a particular IP address. One of the results made the hairs on the back of my neck stand up. An IP address was a UK IP registered to 'D Bester Capital'.

I ran a search on D Bester Capital, sure enough up popped a picture of David, whom I recognised from the AviVector website and my initial open source intel. The website I was on was a small marketing page advertising David Bester's private investment ventures.

Initially it looked as if David had also been hit by the file-uploading helicopter. However, I noticed that the date on the login from the Bester IP address was three days after Richard's IP address. I wondered to myself how that could have happened. Were there two toy helicopters perhaps?

David and Richard entered the dining room, and I shook David's hand while Richard introduced us.

"So, Richard just brought me up to speed with what you've found out so far, it all sounds a bit far-fetched to me. Are you sure this is what happened?"

"It's a new one for me, I'll agree, but it definitely seems like the person who gave you this toy helicopter made some modifications to turn it into an intelligence gathering cyber-weapon."

David shook his head in disbelief, "Incredible", he said.

"Did you get one of these for yourself David?" I asked.

"No, I was given it as a gift, but I knew Richard's boy Chris would love it, that is if he could get it out of Richard's hands to play with the bloody thing!" David smirked.

"That's interesting then, because the server that these files were uploaded to was accessed from an IP address that is registered to your investment company. I assumed it was because you'd been targeted in the same way, but if that's not the case…" David started to turn white in response to my bombshell.

"Oh my, well it looks like I've been attacked by these same people too? Is that what you're saying?" He responded sheepishly.

"Well, that is one explanation. Another is that someone who connects to the Internet from your investment company IP address is behind this whole thing, how many people work in your office?"

"Oh, it's just me. No one else. So, it must be a compromise, right?"

I could tell that a very large penny was dropping inside Richard's brain.

"Dave, was this you?" he said. Suddenly I felt like I was about to play third wheel in an epic scrap between two people who thought they could trust each other.

"What have you been drinking tonight Richard? Of course, I didn't have anything to do with this! What the hell man!"

"It's just you were awfully keen to sell off this contract to VTSD when I called you earlier. You spend a lot of time with them, I just wonder where your loyalties lie here."

"I'm just trying to save the company from going under man, that's all. Jeez."

"So, you wouldn't mind if Parker looks at your laptop then?" Richard asked David.

"What?" He replied.

"If you have nothing to hide, let us take a look at your laptop. We won't find anything if you have nothing that implicates you in this." Richard made a good point, I knew he was smart.

"No, I'm not going to let some guy I just met crawl through my laptop. I have personal stuff on there." It was at this point I decided to jump in.

"This would be very confidential David, I'd sign a legally binding document that ensures we destroy any images we make of your hard drive and I would not share information that wasn't pertinent to this case with Richard." I could see David start to weigh up his options. Every second he hesitated; he made himself look more guilty. I was an independent third party; there was no reason for him not to do this. Unless he was guilty of course. I decided to help him along.

"Of course, Richard, the other thing we could do is get a warrant to search the mail server that was relaying the messages from the 'hacker' group to you earlier. I'm sure we wouldn't see your outside IP address as the true source IP for the mail traffic. Would we?"

David sat down and put his head in his hands. I knew I'd cracked him. Of course, the chances of us getting a search warrant or cooperation to search a French mail server were zero, but he didn't need to know that.

"Ok guys look, Richard, yes this was me, but you need to let me explain why." Richard had a look on his face of sheer rage, but was prepared to hear David out.

"I bought out VTSD the other day. I'm now the owner. Richard, I am going to sell my AviVector stake, and move out to China. It's just that I needed some surety, in the form of a multi-year contract before doing that. I didn't want to find myself out there and SOL if things went wrong."

"So, you thought you'd screw me, our employees and your own brother? Just to make yourself feel a bit more comfortable? Classy."

I rarely got to see these types of confessions play out in front of me like this. It was rather unnerving.

"I know, I'm truly sorry man. We'll sort this out. I promise."

I knew at this point the case was closed as far as I was concerned. These guys would have to sort out the details between them, but I was dying to know who had come up with the idea of the toy helicopter, it was ingenious.

"David, is any of the code still at risk? My advice to you would be to eliminate it from anywhere it resides outside the lab, to protect AviVector from reputational damage, should any outsider stumble upon it."

"I will take care of it." He said.

"Well Richard, I will let you two sort this one out, I have a copy of everything as evidence if you need it, of course."

"Parker, I can't thank you enough for all your work tonight, awesome job. Obviously, although this is a less than ideal scenario, it could have been so much worse."

We shook hands and Richard showed me out. I didn't shake hands with David.

"Let's talk tomorrow, just so I don't spend the entire day wondering if you killed him, okay?" I said, half-jokingly. "Oh, and also we need to discuss the bill, and as long as I charge less than $2.5 million, you can still consider yourself up on where you would have been."

"Sure, I will do that. I mean, I will call you, not kill him." Richard smiled, his relief apparent. He'd even started to get his colour back, although some of that was probably from his rage.

I left the house and headed for home, via the petrol station so I could pick up a sausage roll and some reasonably priced wine to celebrate another job well done. Rock'n'Roll.

Crossbow: Epilogue

I followed up with Richard the next day, he added more colour to what David had been trying to achieve. David had wanted his newly acquired company to have the contract, but felt like he had given enough to AviVector that he shouldn't have to pay for it. He came up with the ransom idea while reading about DDoS ransoms in a technical magazine. VTSD would pay for the contract, but ultimately get the money back via the ransom. Although, Richard and I personally doubted that money would ever find its way back into the VTSD corporate accounts.

David's planning had been meticulous, he'd waited for the security manager's holiday before executing his plan, just so he'd be out of the way. He hadn't counted on Richard calling me.

I asked about the idea to embed file-stealing code into a toy helicopter.

"He was chatting to a young guy in the VTSD Global office, who told him he was a keen hacker. David asked him how to steal data from a system not connected to the Internet, and the guy introduced him to a USB hacksaw." Richard explained. "The hacksaw stole information like passwords when it was inserted into a machine. David asked him to modify it to grab source code. He knew he'd never be able to get me to insert a USB stick, so he came up with the idea to disguise it in a toy helicopter after seeing one charging in the VTSD offices. He knew I'd be a sucker for that. The same kid apparently performed the modification on the USB drive and just wired it into the electronics in the helicopter. Smart kid, wish we'd hired him."

At that point in time they'd decided not to pursue legal action against David, they didn't want information about the episode to get out and cause more problems. Eric Bester had had no knowledge of the plot and wasn't talking to his brother.

AviVector eventually released the Crossbow software and their drone program went on to make more money than they could have expected. Some of the drones they produced cost well over a million quid and were some of the most advanced commercial drones available, and to think, the whole thing could have been curtailed by a tiny toy helicopter!

Oh, and one final thing, AviVector is probably the only company I know of who call out toy helicopters as a prohibited item in their security policies.

Vigilante

Vigilante: Chapter One

"I'm looking at the car right now. It's the BMW five series estate; it's an absolute mess. Yes, the police have been called." I heard the agitated and red-faced executive yell into his mobile as we approached him from behind.

I was walking alongside Tony Arden, head of group security for Dixon-White, a construction conglomerate. We were visiting the home of the latest executive from his company to have been subjected to an attack conducted by an anarchist group.

The group, who took issue with a Dixon-White subsidiary winning a contract to build a facility that would ultimately be used for researching and creating genetically modified foods, had been damaging property belonging to anyone who had their name on the Dixon-White website.

This unfortunate man just had just awoken to find his BMW's Black Sapphire paint job transformed into a custom "Black Sapphire with dribbles of paint stripper artfully poured all over the roof" one. Needless to say, he didn't seem to like it. He ended his phone call and turned to us.

"Tony, what are you doing to stop these bastards? This is ridiculous. I don't even have anything to do with this project they're pissed off about. I assume the company is paying my excess?"

"Alan, I'm sorry this happened, we are working with the police to catch those responsible. It is a top priority for them."

"Yeah, well, we all know how quickly the police move in this area, so hopefully they'll have caught them before I retire." The man looked at me. I introduced myself and apologised for the loss of his beloved metallic overcoat.

"Parker is going to be assisting us with some elements of the investigation, he's a computer security and investigation expert." Tony explained.

"Well, I'd prefer the company spend money on a 'locate and beat the shit out of them' expert, but whatever."

We took some pictures of the damage to the car, spoke to the local policeman who arrived to record the crime, and headed back to the offices of Dixon-White, some thirty-five miles away.

I'd been hired by Dixon-White because this type of attack, along with various other forms of unpleasantness, had been going on for about a month and they wanted my assistance in breaking the chain. The police criminal investigations department were involved, of course, but limited resources seemed to be frustrating leadership at Dixon-White. They wanted to protect their staff, and also wrap up the contact.

Dixon-White and the police both believed the group were very active online. Be it planning or promoting their agenda. They wanted me to try and find if that was the case, through open source intelligence gathering. The idea being that evidence located could help Dixon-White direct the police and their internal security resources to be in the right place at the right time.

Another objective I'd been given was to identify the key players hosting communications about the attacks, so that civil legal proceedings could begin.

I was in the middle of my initial meeting with Tony Arden when the call came in about the latest incident, which had forced us to jump in his car to go and take a look. Once we'd gotten back to his office, we were able to pick up where we'd left off.

"Parker, what you saw there was just one example of what these guys are doing, and they are doing it to people that have no involvement in this project whatsoever. It's simply a case of guilty by association to Dixon-White." Tony said.

He went on to explain in more detail some of the other 'unpleasantness' experienced by his staff members he mentioned earlier.

"We've had a guy who got feces through the post, in another case it was a used tampon - can you believe that? Disgusting. And then, there is all the psychological stuff they've been doing. Threatening phone calls at all hours of the day, anonymous emails with much the same. We even have a guy whose neighbours were contacted by post. The letter alleged that he was a paedophile and that his neighbours should be aware. The poor guy has no criminal convictions whatsoever, and in his case, this was the first he knew of any of this."

I was shocked. I understand people get passionate about the things they believe in, but I don't think anyone in the right frame of mind could really justify doing these kinds of things to other human beings. Especially human beings, who for the most part, were not even aware of the project that was being objected to.

"So where is the police investigation at?" I asked.

"The police have been doing the best they can, they've spent the night outside of the homes of a couple of our people after being tipped off that they might be next. They are pursuing the traditional police investigation route, but what they are lacking are resources and consequently, speed. They have some names that they are watching closely, but no real evidence that they can tie back to an individual. Apparently, the anarchist group is newly formed, which is only serving to make investigating them more difficult."

"Understood. So, what I'm going to need is everything that you currently know about this group. I need copies of emails received, any recordings or transcripts of the threatening phone calls. I want as clear a picture as I can get of who I'm investigating."

Tony reached for the keychain on his belt, and opened a deep drawer in his desk. He pulled out a black binder, and handed it to me.

"This is everything I've collated so far. The group goes by the name of 'Stop Smuthernature'. All emails are signed off with that name."

I started to flick through the binder; one thing I noticed immediately was that only the body of the email messages were recorded, not any of the header information.

"I see these emails were sent to Dixon-White addresses, do you have an on-site email server? Would someone be able to provide me with access to the log files? I'd like to be able to see where the sending infrastructure is located."

"I'm afraid I don't have the answer to that, you'll have to have a chat with our IT manager, Rebecca Shaw, she'll probably be a good person for you to meet anyway. Let me see if I can find her, hang tight for a minute." Tony exited his office, leaving me alone with the binder while he went to try and locate Rebecca.

I continued to browse through the evidence in front of me. The contents of the emails were plain nasty. I read one aloud to myself.

"GOD cannot be replaced by GMO. Dixon-White, you filthy bastards, stop construction of this house of playing God, or you won't ever build anything again. It's hard to build anything when you're dead."

The sending address of that email was clearly spoofed, and having reviewed about a dozen more of the hard copy emails in the binder it appeared that the sending addresses were just randomly generated. This was somewhat important initial information. It let me know that there was some technical skill behind the emails. It wasn't just a case of someone setting up a bunch of free email accounts, and using them to send messages. This also eliminated one line of enquiry right there; it wouldn't be possible to go to a free email provider with a warrant asking for access logs to be released.

Tony re-entered the room accompanied by someone who I assumed was Rebecca, the IT manager. I was right. After a brief introduction in Tony's office, I walked with Rebecca down the hall to her department offices. Tony had another meeting so I'd agreed to call him the following day to discuss where I was at in the investigation.

After spending just a few minutes discussing things with Rebecca, I had determined she was one of the better IT managers I'd ever had to work with. She was relatively young, perhaps mid-twenties, and commanded a great deal of respect from her team of five. That team was comprised of three technicians and two senior technicians. She had been at the company for about four years, worked her way up the ladder and as a result had a great deal of intimate knowledge of the Dixon-White networks and IT infrastructure.

Dixon-White did not have an information security team, so it was down to Rebecca and her crew to dabble in everything from fixing printers to firewall management. It turned out that information security was a favourite topic of Rebecca's, and an area she wanted to move into in the future.

"One day I'll convince them to let me do information security work full time, once the company is a bit bigger," she said.

Rebecca was fully briefed on why I was working with Dixon-White, and she had first-hand knowledge of the threatening emails I'd just read. She'd even taken steps to prevent some of the emails from reaching her colleagues.

"Every time a new one comes in we block the sending address, but of course, they always change it, so it's pretty pointless. We're also trialling a profanity filter."

I asked Rebecca if she could provide me with the transport logs for the threatening emails.

"Yes, I can grab those for you, we run our own Microsoft Exchange system here. It'll just be a few minutes."

There were a few minutes of generic IT security chatter while she worked at extracting the logs and copying them to my external USB drive, after which Rebecca showed me out of the building.

"I really hope you can help them find out who is behind this. My good friend who had worked here for almost two years quit last week because she was afraid. She worked in accounting for God's sake! Please, keep me in the loop and let me know if there is anything I can do to help."

"Will do," I promised Rebecca as I shook her hand. "Thanks again for your help, it was great meeting you."

Vigilante: Chapter Two

Back in my lab, sipping on a cup of Tetley tea, I once again commenced perusal of the binder provided to me by Tony Arden.

I fired up a copy of a software tool called Maltego. It's my absolute favourite tool for this kind of work. It allows you to draw out diagrams connecting different entities, such as people or domain names, together when a relationship is discovered. A bit like a detective connecting pictures of the major players in a crime together on a whiteboard.

It even does clever things like automatically scour the Internet for email addresses and user profiles when names are entered. Maltego would be the repository for information discovered during the open source enumeration exercise. Of course, the first step was to find some things to deposit in Maltego.

At this point, I had a collection of threatening emails, around thirty in total, and all the associated log information for those emails. I also had a name the group was using, Stop Smuthernature.

Turning my attention to the email logs, I examined the three 'hops' taken by the mail prior to its arrival in the unfortunate recipient's inbox. The final IP was a private IP, the internal Dixon-White server where mail was stored, the IP before that was an external IP address that belonged to another Dixon-White server, which I assumed given the hostname was some sort of mail gateway that did all of the talking with the outside world. The final IP was the sending IP. The IP address of the server that had relayed the message to Dixon-White. I noticed that of the thirty emails, three different sending IP's were used.

I proceeded to look up information on those IP's using online 'whois' records, which contain information on the organisation that has been assigned a particular block of IP address space, and by using my trusty assistant Mr. Google.

The first appeared to belong to a Belgian University, and was simply an open SMTP relay. In other words, a poorly configured email server that was willing to forward email on behalf of anyone who wanted it to do so.

It was the same story for the second and third sending IP's. One was associated with a virtual private server hosted by a Dutch hosting company, and the other appeared to be a Russian hosting company.

So, three open SMTP relays were used to send the messages to Dixon-White. Not really a surprise, and not really much to go on as far as my investigation was concerned.

Still looking at the email logs, I wanted to get an idea of the time of day that the email messages were sent. I was looking for a pattern; did the sender or senders prefer to send the messages at a particular time of day? Did they prefer a particular day of the week? Questions like this can help one determine the level of access to computing equipment the perpetrator has.

I imported the log files into a spreadsheet, extracted the receive timestamps and sorted them to make sure they were in order. The emails had been sent in clusters over the course of the past three weeks, and I did detect a bit of a pattern. The emails were always sent in threes, one from each of the three open email relays, about four minutes apart.

Moreover, they always appeared on Mondays between two and three o'clock in the afternoon, Wednesdays between eleven and one o'clock in the afternoon and also Friday mornings between half past nine and half past ten. Nothing at all on weekends and nothing in the evenings. I needed to know more before I could start to build assumptions based on this finding, but it was still intriguing.

I filed the email transmission pattern in the back of my mind and turned my attention away from the email logs. I wanted to look at the email content.

There was no doubt, of course, that whoever was ultimately behind the emails was a domestic actor. The physical property damage that had occurred within the UK was evidence enough of that. However, I did note that all of the emails appeared to be in well-formed English. There was no broken English, or poor grammar. This only served to solidify in my mind that the sender probably spoke English as a first language, and was probably reasonably smart. Well, as smart as one can be if they're engaged in sending threatening emails to innocent people.

A common theme that the sender kept coming back to in the emails was that the facility under construction would provide a home for scientists who would be 'playing God' and 'trying to improve upon God's perfect work'. This was a more prevalent theme than, for example, possible environmental damage or changes caused by genetically modified food. This led me to question the real motivation of the sender. Was this more of an extreme religious actor, rather than someone who was solely an environmentalist? All information was noted before turning my attention to the second piece of evidence.

I Googled "stop smuthernature" and started to peruse the results. Very little came up. There was a news story from a local village newspaper, which was related to some property damage that occurred in said village. The garage door at the home of Dixon-White Marketing Director, Claire McGowan had been covered in red paint, and the local rag had run the story so that folks in the village knew what was going on.

In the story, the reporter had referenced the group name, hence the Google news hit. That was the only story that referenced the group name.

I continued to browse through the results, not finding anything particularly interesting, until one caught my eye. It was a forum, and one of the usernames was smuthernature. Coincidence? I wasn't sure, so I opened the link to the page.

The forum was an online farming community, ripe with discussion about everything from crops to tractors. Okay, so I can't take credit for that pun, 'ripe with discussion' was actually forum's tag line.

Smuthernature had about a dozen posts on the forum, most seemed sensible and level-headed enough. However, crucially, they were all about genetically modified foods. Although this was of course extremely interesting to me, I was still a million miles away from connecting the forum user to the person or persons sending abusive emails to Dixon-White employees.

I reviewed the user profile for Smuthernature. It contained limited information. No email address was visible publicly and all I could see were the total number of posts by the user. There was an option to send the user a direct message, so I clicked on it, in the hope that it might reveal some contact information. I was instantly redirected to a page that informed me that I'd need to sign up to send a forum user a message. So, I did just that.

A couple of minutes later, 'FarmerGiles' had become the latest member of the forum. He had a throwaway email address, of course, and thanks to the TOR anonymous Internet browser installed on my system had a Swiss IP address.

Under my new pseudonym, I returned to the profile page of Smuthernature. Although no further contact information was visible, a new piece of the profile had become available. Smuthernature had an avatar.

The avatar was an image shown in a reduced size format on the profile page. I right clicked on the image to copy the image URL, which I then pasted into another browser tab. The URL structure made it very easy for me to forcefully browse to the image in its original size. I promptly downloaded it to review it in more detail. I know, forceful browsing to an image file was just about on the cusp of what could be considered real open source information gathering, but sometimes you just have to live a little.

It was a computer-generated graphic of a black skull and crossbones munching on a piece of green and yellow corn.

This graphic did not appear in any of the emails or other materials that Tony Arden had provided to me, so I sent him a quick email with the file attached, and asked him if he'd seen it before.

While I waited for the response from Tony, I sat back in my chair and stared at the graphic now filling the screen in front of me. Could this graphic have been produced on the very same piece of hardware being used to send the threatening emails to the folks at Dixon-White? My heart started to race a little at the prospect, and I lunged forward to try and find a way to figure that out.

The image file was in the JPEG file format. A file format commonly found on the Internet, of course, and one that more often than not contains a lot more information than just the contents of the image itself. JPEG files can sometimes contain a great deal of valuable metadata, stored in a format called exchangeable image file format, or EXIF for short. In my primary web browser, I have an add-on, which allows me to right click on any image and view any associated EXIF data.

The contents of EXIF data can be wide ranging. Everything from technical details about the camera that took a photograph such as the lens type and serial number, to information about the photographer. Some newer devices, particularly smartphones, even log the location of a photograph in the form of GPS coordinates!

It's possible to strip the EXIF data from a file, so there were no guarantees that there would be any, and even if there were, it might not be useful at all.

I right clicked, and the add-on did its magic. Up popped a few lines of EXIF metadata from the graphic.

There was no smoking gun. Nothing that told me, 'this graphic was produced by Mr. X at X location', but one thing did stand out as interesting. The graphic was put together on Adobe Photoshop Elements for Macintosh, a sort of lower cost version of the infamous Photoshop software. So, I now knew that whoever made that graphic did so on Elements, and had a Mac. All very good, but I was still no closer to working out who they were, and if they were connected in any way to the case I was investigating.

An email notification popped up on my screen, it was a reply from Tony Arden. It was brilliant news.

"Parker, yes, I have seen this image before. It was on a malicious letter sent to our Managing Director early on, but unfortunately, we didn't keep a copy of that letter. At that point, we just dismissed it as someone playing a joke. Of course, in hindsight, we shouldn't have done that," the email read.

Although it was a shame I couldn't see the contents of that letter, it didn't really matter. I had my first confirmation that there was some link between the user of this forum, and in particular the graphic he was using as an avatar and the person threatening Dixon-White.

That was all very well and good, and a huge breakthrough, but I was well aware I needed more. I needed to find out all the other places this user and image were on the Internet.

I have tens of thousands of pounds' worth of legally admissible, court-approved hardware and software in my lab. I have a rack full of servers that can take terabytes of data and index it all out for me overnight, but right now all I needed, was Google.

In particular, I'd recently been made aware of a new feature in Google's image search product. It was like a reverse image search, instead of looking for an image by typing a keyword, you could upload an image and find other images that looked like it and sites that hosted the same image you'd uploaded.

I dragged the Smuthernature graphic into the Google tool, and got one hit back. At first, I assumed that this was probably the forum that I'd found the image. Then I remembered, I had to authenticate to get that image, so there was no way that Google would have indexed it. I was right, an image, exactly the same as the one I had appeared on an entirely different website.

I drew my first relationship in Maltego. An image file on a forum was linked to a threatening letter, and appeared on another website. An hour ago, I had nothing, but now, using nothing but open source information found on the Internet, I had the beginnings of my investigation. Of course, part of me was thinking, couldn't the police really have found the time to do this?

Oh well, I guess if they'd have bothered I would have been missing out on all the fun!

Vigilante: Chapter Three

I began to look at the second site hosting the Smuthernature avatar graphic. The page itself appeared to belong to a group called 'The Only Way is Organic' who described themselves as a group that a non-profit organisation set up to promote and encourage farms to adopt organic farming methods.

This was interesting. The web page was full of contact information for seemingly real people, event details and blog posts. It all looked very above board. If I had stumbled upon this site during the course of normal browsing, I wouldn't have thought twice about the motivations of its owners. However, I was troubled by the fact that the Smuthernature avatar was present on one of the pages.

The page it was featured on was actually an advertisement for an event, a protest rally outside parliament in London. According to the page, the group was protesting a newly passed law that would see companies performing certain experiments with genetically modified foods getting tax breaks. The date of the rally had actually already passed, some six weeks ago.

There was an interesting line at the bottom of the page.

"Remember, our protests are legal and peaceful, we do not encourage those joining us to break the law and we request that everyone follow the instructions of the police."

The avatar graphic certainly didn't look peaceful. It was an interesting choice for this group to use on their webpage.

I downloaded a new copy of the image, this time from the protest group page. I reviewed the EXIF data to determine if this was truly the same image file.

The exact same EXIF data was present. The image was produced on Adobe Photoshop Elements on a Mac.

For the sake of being one hundred per cent sure, I ran both images through an MD5 hash generator. If the two hash values were the same, there would be absolutely no doubt that these two files were the exact same thing, and not subtly different. We had a perfect match.

This was incredible information. The question now was, did the person on the forum simply grab the image from the protest group page, or did they create the image themselves?

I continued to peruse the protest group's website. On one of the pages, something caught my eye. It was the 'contact us' page.

The group had a public PGP key available, for anyone that wanted to send them an encrypted email message. Nothing wrong with this at all of course, but it did stand out as slightly unusual. Why would this group be so concerned about email security? I read further down the page, and my question was answered.

"If you are a whistle-blower, the PGP key will allow you to send us messages in the utmost confidence that they will be secure and private."

This group just got a tad more exciting! I thought they were just into farming methods, but apparently, they work with whistle-blowers. Interesting.

I noted all the contact information and a generated a site map in Maltego for the latest site. I then ran a couple of technical "transforms" as Maltego calls them, to discover more about the hosting infrastructure behind the site. Transforms are essentially little automated jobs that expedite the process of looking things up manually on the command line. All still open source information, of course.

The website was hosted on a server with a Swedish IP address, which belonged to a virtual private server hosting company. These types of services are common, you pay a company to host a virtual machine, which you can use to host whatever you want.

What is not so common, was for a group based solely in the UK, according to their website, to use facilities in Sweden to host that very website. Of course, the Internet is a truly global thing, it doesn't really matter where you put things, it's just the normal approach that one does business with those in the same country as you, to eliminate problems such as currency exchange or language barriers.

Whenever I'm studying a website hosted on a virtual private server and I want to know more about its hosting arrangements, I have a very simple trick, and this time it has nothing to do with Google. It's Bing.

The search engine Bing has a very cool feature that I have yet to find the equivalent of in Google. You can enter "ip" followed by a colon, and then the IP address of a server. Bing will tell you about all the domains hosted on that IP that it knows about. If you get back hundreds of results, chances are that the server is a truly multi-tenant deal, where customers pay just for web space on a communal server to plonk their websites.

However, if you get a handful of results, it's usually a dedicated server rented by an individual to host only their sites, or the sites of their clients.

In the case of this Swedish virtual private server, I got four results. The protest group site was one of them; the second and third results appeared to be other sites related to the same subject matter. The final hit was by far the most interesting.

The domain name included the word "smuther", spelled as it had been in the emails and online forum. It wasn't as obvious as going to stopsmuthernature.com for example, but it wasn't far off.

I went to click on the link, but thought better of it at the last second. This was potentially a server belonging to a suspect; I have a business grade Internet connection with a static IP address. It was attributable to me. I needed to use TOR to access this site, and in fact any of the others hosted on the same infrastructure from now on.

In my TOR browser, I made my first tentative steps on the "smuther" site, the experience made all the more tense by the reduced performance on TOR.

The site was actually pretty plain. The now familiar avatar graphic was present at the top of every page. It was a simple, basic HTML website with three links on the side.

"Mission. News. Contact."

The mission page included a brief introduction to the group. I was still buzzing at the fact that I'd just discovered that they had such a visible online presence. Although it was tucked away in a little corner of cyberspace, with clearly few direct links, it was still out there for all to see.

"Stop Smuthernature is a direct-action anarchist group who work to bring down corporations and individuals associated with the disgusting and downright wrong business of playing with our God-given food supply," the page read.

The news section was lengthier, and much to my surprise featured information about the campaign against Dixon-White. Several members of staff and their home addresses were listed on the website, below their information there was a call to action.

"These are employees of Dixon-White, the company currently building a facility that will ultimately ensure that genetically modified food steps into the mainstream. While we have plans for them, we encourage any of you who support our cause to visit the homes of these bastards and do as you will. They have all been warned. They don't have to work for this organisation."

Scrolling down the chronographically arranged list of news updates, there were more specific details about the deeds committed by the group.

"Last night we attacked the home of Dixon-White employee Claire McGowan. How do you like that bitch?! The outside of your home is covered in red, just like the blood of those who will die as a result of the destruction of the natural food supply."

These guys were openly admitting to the crime on their website. They wanted people to know that they meant business.

I scrolled down. More names and contact details of employees to be targeted. This time, I noticed a name I was familiar with. Rebecca Shaw, the IT manager I'd met earlier. They didn't have her address thankfully, but they did have a home phone number.

As I continued to scroll down through the page I came across a couple of photographs of cars covered in paint stripper, and other similar property damage. I was quick to download the photos. Remember the EXIF data we discussed earlier? I wanted to know if there was any lingering data on these images for sure.

I downloaded the photos to my machine for EXIF inspection. I was excited to see a gargantuan blob of EXIF data, which I knew would probably justify my fee for the case alone.

The EXIF data stopped short of giving me the name and address of the person that took the photo, but it gave me pretty much every other detail that I could ever want to know. More importantly, every detail the police would surely like to know about the moment the person pressed the shutter button to take a picture of the crime they just committed.

I checked the second photo. It had the same camera model, and same serial number.

All the details were promptly copied into my notes and I resumed the search for more information. Although I now knew intimately the camera hardware used by someone at the scene of one of the crimes committed against a couple of Dixon-White employees, I still needed to try and get an idea as to whom that someone was.

Something was bugging me though. I remembered that my earlier assumption was the person who was sending the threatening emails showed signs of being technically savvy. Surely a person who knew enough to send a message through an open email relay, would be smart enough to remember to strip the EXIF data out of an image of a crime scene they'd just created?

This was an anarchist group, and a group consists of more than one. Perhaps the paint stripper attacks are handled by one team, while the other, more sensible team hid online and abused people electronically.

In my head, I went back to the fact that the anarchist group page and protest group page were resident on the same dedicated virtual server.

I didn't think for one second this was coincidence. I was certain that there was a relationship between the supposed peaceful group and the anarchists. Even if both groups were just getting hosting support from the server owner, it was still a link.

I started to compile a summary report of everything that I'd discovered so far, including the names of everyone linked to the The Only Way is Organic protest group. This was emailed to Tony Arden and also Rebecca Shaw. I knew she'd be interested to see what I'd been able to discover so far. No more than fifteen minutes later, Tony Arden called me.

"This is incredible work Parker, I'm blown away by how much you can find, if you know how to look for it."

I thanked him for his kind words.

"Do you have any names associated with the group?"

I explained to Tony that I had pulled names openly associated with the peaceful protest group, but that I had no way of confirming they were involved in the anarchist group. Still, it was likely worth the police asking them questions.

"Listen, tomorrow I am expecting a visit from a member of the police counter terrorism unit. He is acting as liaison for us during the case. Can you come and join us to discuss your findings, perhaps show us these websites and talk more about the names you've found?"

"I'll be there," I responded. I was pleased to hear that a counter terrorism officer was now involved, as in my opinion what this group was doing was essentially domestic terrorism.

I ended my call with Tony, and noticed I had an email response from Rebecca.

"Oh Lord, my number is on their website. I haven't had any strange calls yet, but I doubt it'll be long. I just hope my daughter doesn't answer the phone if it rings. Thanks for the information!"

Vigilante: Chapter Four

The next morning, I headed back to the offices of Dixon-White. I had hard copies of my findings, along with a couple of CD's with electronic copies of the same. The CD's and hard copies contained the summary report, which included my relationship diagram produced in Maltego. After a bit of chitchat with the receptionist I was escorted into Tony's office, where I found him and another gentleman in a suit.

"Parker, come on in, this is Detective Robert Hallam, he's been assigned to us from the Counter Terrorism unit of our regional police force." The detective stood up and we shook hands.

"So, Parker, how about you take us through your findings from yesterday, and we'll jump in with any questions that may come up," Tony instructed, handing me a VGA cable so I could project onto his wall using a desktop projector that had been moved into position.

I began to run through my work from yesterday, a step-by-step reproduction, explaining the relationships between the various websites, how I came across the avatar, and finding the serial number of the camera from the crime scene photos in the EXIF data. The detective took notes throughout.

"Can you bring up these websites for us now, to take a look at?" the detective enquired.

"Certainly." I explained that I would connect to the sites using my mobile broadband hotspot, to eliminate the risk of any traffic being traced back to the offices of Dixon-White, although Tony Arden didn't seem overly concerned about that anyway.

"They obviously want our staff to see the messages on the site and be intimidated, so it'll probably give them a thrill if they can see we're the ones looking at it."

I browsed to the website belonging to The Only Way is Organic protest group. My browser hung for a while, before returning a "404 page not found" error. Weird, I thought, I was sure I typed in the correct URL. I verified it and tried again.

"This is strange, I'm sorry, let me try the other site." I entered the URL for the stop smuthernature direct action site. The same thing happened. A server side 404-error message. You may recall, that I'd seen two other sites on this server. I tried to hit those too, but again was presented with a 404 error.

"Well, it looks like those pages have gone away, perhaps they're updating the server or performing some other maintenance," I explained.

"Never mind, we have screenshots and these are really useful, I'll try and access the sites later on," Hallam said.

The detective said that they planned on bringing in a couple of the names I'd handed over for questioning over the next couple of days.

"This name has come up before, and so has this one," he said, pointing to the names printed on the paper in front of him.

I agreed with Tony that I'd be available should they want me to provide more information, or do any follow up work. I left his office and started to make my way back to the reception area to hand in my visitor badge. I felt a tap on my shoulder; I turned around to see Rebecca Shaw, the IT manager.

"Hi there Rebecca, how are you doing today?"

"I'm good thanks Parker, that was really interesting info you sent over about those websites yesterday. I'd love to be doing that as a job!" I suspected she was about to ask if I was going to be hiring anytime soon.

"So, did you notice, the sites aren't there this morning?" she asked.

"Erm… yes, I just found out about that, did you try and browse to the sites as well?"

"Well. Let's just say, I really didn't care for my number being on there, nor any of the numbers belonging to any of my colleagues and friends… and now they aren't, so that's good." She smiled.

I didn't really know what to make of this comment. It took a while for it to sink in.

"Rebecca, did you… I mean, did you… bring the sites down?" I asked.

She smiled back at me.

"Want me to show you how?" She beckoned me to her area of the office. I stood there for a while. My heart was racing. Rebecca, although full of good intentions for sure, had just committed a crime, and was about to show me how she did it! To say I felt a little conflicted and unsure of what to do next was an understatement, so I figured I'd follow her and see what she was about to show me.

The IT office was empty, so Rebecca talked aloud.

"So, since you already did the enumeration for me, I figured I'd move on to doing the more active stuff." Rebecca spoke like someone familiar with the traditional hacking methodology.

"So, I ran a port scan, discovered an open FTP service on the server and then figured I'd run a brute force attack against the username admin."

She opened up a copy of the password-cracking tool Brutus AE2. Brutus was a basic, but effective tool for running brute force or dictionary based password attacks against protocols such as HTTP, FTP or POP3.

Rebecca showed me run logs from Brutus. The logs showed me that she'd run a dictionary attack against the FTP service on the server and had, within about 15 minutes, cracked the admin user password as it was weak and based on a simple dictionary word.

With that password, she'd been able to login to the server and delete all of the content from the web root. All the HTML files and images were gone, and as a result of that, the sites were effectively down.

The demonstration concluded, and I was unsure of what to say.

"Well, I mean, clearly the folks running this site weren't overly concerned about security... but Rebecca, from my perspective, this puts me in a somewhat awkward position." I sat back in the chair and threw my head back, wondering what my next step should be.

From a human perspective, I agreed with some elements of Rebecca's activity. From a professional perspective, I knew she'd broken the law and had taken the actions of someone I'd usually spend time chasing down. I wanted to help her out of the mess, but how could I without incriminating myself, or getting her in deeper.

"So where did you run this attack from? Were you behind a proxy or anything?"

"Oh, no I just ran it from here." She replied.

"Ah, so when you broke in, did you obtain access to any log files, you know... so you could cover your tracks?"

"No, I didn't."

So now there was potentially evidence that a Dixon-White IP had conducted a destructive hack on the server of an anarchist group that was not afraid of breaking the law. If the anarchists had issues with Dixon-White before, they surely would now.

I pondered for a few more seconds, and I arrived at a decision.

"Rebecca, I think we need to get back in there and see if we can trash some logs."

Maybe it was my natural instinct to protect people like her kicking in, or maybe it was my desire to see if I could discover more about this group by looking at the innards of their server, but I was about to do something I swore I'd never do. I was about to help someone who was technically a malicious hacker, cover her tracks. What had been a simple open source intelligence investigation some minutes earlier, had taken a somewhat surprising twist.

At this point I wasn't sure if I should speak to Tony Arden. I felt as if he should be briefed on these latest developments, both from a security perspective, as there was now an increased likelihood of retaliatory attacks and from a client relationship perspective, as he was the person who engaged me initially.

"Rebecca, I think we need to discuss this with Tony first. I just want him to understand what is going on."

Rebecca was concerned at first, but eventually agreed that it was the right move. She was also apologetic, sort of.

"Parker, while I can't say I'm sorry for doing this, I'm sorry I did this in a way that you believe increases the risk to our folks. I was just getting so frustrated at how long they were taking to do anything."

We headed across to Tony's office. Tony was surprised to see that I was still around. By now, the detective had left, thankfully.

"Tony, I've found the reason we couldn't access those sites earlier," I pointed at Rebecca. "You've got a vigilante in the organisation."

"I'm sorry Tony, I was just so worried, I wanted to take my phone number off the site, and protect my daughter, and I got carried away."

I summarised the current state of play for Tony. Explaining that legally, nothing would likely come of this. I mean it is unlikely that if you're hosting a server full of evidence about criminal acts, you're going to hand it over to the police so that they can investigate your own complaint. However, we wanted to go back in and do some cover up work.

"Ok Parker, you seem to know what you're doing here. So, let's get that taken care of, I agree. And Rebecca, I see why you did what you did. I'd have probably done the same if I knew how!"

And with that, Rebecca and I headed to a quiet corner of the IT area and opened an FTP connection to the server. This time hopping through a chain of proxy servers, thanks to the TOR network.

The now empty web root was our landing point as the FTP connection completed. I went up a directory and began to have a look around. Much to my joy, it was extremely easy to find the FTP logs. They were in a folder with HTTP logs.

"So just hit delete, and it's gone, right Parker?" Rebecca eagerly asked.

"Well, since we've already broken the law, it probably won't make much difference to do a little bit more and grab a copy of these logs. They could have some useful intelligence about who manages this site."

I copied off the logs, and performed a quick review. I wanted to validate that no one had logged into the server after Rebecca's deletion spree. If they had, we were probably too late.

Thankfully, for the evening into the morning the logs were full of Dixon-White IP's and no others. With a copy safely saved on my machine, I pressed delete on the original logs, validated they'd disappeared, closed the connection and received a hug from Rebecca.

"Thank you for that, I probably wouldn't have been able to sleep if we'd not done that. I can't believe I didn't think about covering my tracks," she said.

"Well, let's never talk about it again. It's done now."

"So, what of the log files, what can you tell about who is accessing this server on a regular basis?" she asked.

I'd hoped to be able to review the logs in the comfort of my lab, perhaps with a stiff drink in hand, but of course, the ever-eager Rebecca had other ideas.

We began to look through the logs together. There were a couple of IP addresses that were persistently connecting to the FTP connection, to upload new content to the sites. The first IP address appeared to have been used consistently up until about a week ago, then it switched to a new IP. I dropped the first non Dixon-White IP from the logs into Google. It, of course, was a known anonymous proxy server out of the Ukraine. Not much intelligence to be had there.

The second IP, which was the most recent to login aside from the Dixon-White IP's, did however resolve somewhere altogether more interesting. It was a British IP, and belonged to an extremely prestigious private school if the 'whois' record was to be believed.

I had a lot of contacts in the local education world, from a prior job back in the early part of my career. I didn't know if any of my contacts were directly involved in supporting that school, or if they knew who was, but I figured it was worth a shot.

I wanted to get permission from Tony first, so I briefed him on our current status.

"Tony, the logs have been deleted. We checked, and we don't think anyone will be the wiser as to what happened. There will still potentially be firewall logs that the service provider has access too, but usually in my experience, they don't retain them for very long."

"Okay, that's great. Thanks for the update Parker." Tony was clearly a bit more comfortable with everything at this point.

"One more thing, we have some intelligence from the server that I'd like to follow up on. Some of the IP addresses used to manage the contents of the server track back to Ketchfield Manor Comprehensive. We think that someone is using their connection. I'd like to brief them, and have them see if they have a mechanism to track it down further. Would that be okay?"

Tony was agreeable; however, he did have some reservations.

"That's fine, but suppose it is someone there and we find them, does it matter that we acquired the evidence linking them to the crime in a somewhat illegal manner?" he asked.

"Leave that part to me," I replied, which was really my way of saying "I hadn't figured that out just yet."

While driving back to the lab I made contact with a friend of mine who did have a good contact for the network administrator at Ketchfield Manor Comprehensive School.

"Oh, that school is managed by David Abbott, he's a top bloke, I can give you his details without a problem," came the response from my connection.

Of course, although he may be considered a 'top bloke' one must always assume the worst-case scenario. This man had unrestricted access to the network that was connecting to our anarchist server, how were we to know that he was not an anarchist himself?

I did some research, checked out arrest records and looked at his online profiles. Nothing but a whole load of posts about getting school software to work. I was satisfied that he was clean.

I called David Abbott and introduced myself. He was interested in what I had to say, and seemed willing to help out. I explained that we'd come into contact with some evidence linking the network he managed with the management of a server being investigated for links to an anarchist group. Of course, I didn't really go into detail about how we'd come across into that evidence.

"Mmmm… what intrigues me most is that you say an anonymous proxy was used up until a few days ago, and then our IP address was used. We recently installed new proxy boxes to block the kids from using external anonymous proxies. They were using them to beat our filtering software so they could play games and watch porn," Dave explained, with disgust.

This was great evidence and the timing added up perfectly. Someone in the school manages the site through an anonymous proxy, suddenly can't access that proxy, and then just decides to use the direct Internet connection. Seems like they got a bit cocky.

I asked Dave if there was a way he could review logs for access to the IP, and if that would allow him to determine who was accessing the server.

"Yes, I can look at that for you. I'll probably have to discuss with the headmaster first, but if he says it's fine, I'll take a look. One thing I can tell you, is that the external IP address you're seeing is on our student network, not our office network."

I thanked Dave for his information and we exchanged contact details.

I began to review my case notes while waiting on a response from Dave. One thing that hit me while doing this was the pattern of threatening emails I'd noted earlier. Monday, Wednesday and Friday, during the day, nothing on weekends. That would fit the profile of a student at school. The well-formed English used in those emails, fit the profile of someone who was attending this school. Surely, this wasn't the work of a group of destructive rich kids?

The phone rang. It was Dave.

"Parker, I've spoken to the head and we've done some investigation. We've identified a student who we believe to be the one responsible for accessing that server. What the head would like to do is have you come over to chat about the case a bit more, so he can understand exactly what is going on. Needless to say, he is taking this very seriously. He'd like you to visit today if you can."

The school was about sixty miles from my lab, and it was already early afternoon. Still, I had to get over there. I couldn't wait on this. I told Dave I'd be over in about an hour and a half.

I called Tony Arden at Dixon-White to inform him of the developments while I drove over to the school. He was happy to know things were moving quickly, and requested that I keep him informed.

I arrived at the school; it was an eighteenth century building with red brickwork mostly covered in climbing plants.

I walked into the foyer, cleared the secretary's stringent security check and waited outside the headmaster's office. I felt like I was twelve again, although I can honestly say the school I attended didn't look a thing like this.

The headmaster was everything I'd imagined him to look like while waiting outside of his office. Mr. D. Steeds, Headmaster, read the name on his door. He had perfectly groomed facial hair. Not one whisker was out of place. His face was big and red. It was obvious that a daily glass of scotch was high on his agenda, or so I imagined.

Dave Abbott was also present in the office; he was a slightly thinner version of the headmaster, with less discipline in his beard, and a few grey hairs poking out like moray eels poking out of a coral formation.

"Mr. Foss, I thank you for bringing this issue to our attention. In all honesty, your phone call to Mr. Abbott has helped us address a number of questions regarding a student of ours," the headmaster explained. "The student, whose name I will not release at the moment, has had behavioural issues this year. We've caught him sneaking around the computer rooms alone multiple times, which is against our rules. He is highly skilled on the computer, but gets bored easily, which could very well be what has taken him down this road. Previously, apart from the odd flick round the ear every once in a while, for speaking out of turn, he has been well behaved."

I asked the head if there is a reason that this student would be protesting genetically modified foods, and also if he believed the student was involved in the property damage.

"I don't believe this student has any beliefs about much outside of his little world, however, his elder brother, a former student at this school whom I remember well is a different story."

The head explained to me that the boy's brother had been a part of many protest groups, and had a need to destroy things.

"I suspect, that the younger boy is simply acting on the orders of his brother to manage this website and send these horrific emails to your client." The headmaster continued, "If I remember correctly, the family owns an organic farming business. I would imagine that in some way the brother is trying to do what he thinks his right by his family, but is going about it in very much the wrong way."

I asked another question, this time it was aimed at Dave Abbott, the network administrator.

"Dave, do you use Apple Macs here?"

"Yes, we do."

"Great, do you use Adobe Photoshop Elements on those Macs?"

"Yes, the students use that."

My line of questioning was of course in relation to the EXIF data associated with the smuthernature avatar. It was just another piece of the puzzle that fell into place.

By now it sounded like we had a pretty strong link and I knew all that was left for me to do was connect Tony Arden and the Detective with the school, and consequently the suspect student.

I called Tony to pass on the details, and left the school a happy man, excited to be heading home. Much like I did when I was a schoolboy.

Vigilante: Epilogue

I met up with Tony Arden in a local pub a few weeks later to discuss the case over a drink and a burger. The schoolboy, fourteen years old, had pretty much caved when challenged about his involvement in the campaign against Dixon-White.

It was as the headmaster had suspected. The boy's brother, who was nineteen, had come up with the idea to start a direct-action protest group called Stop Smuthernature, after reading the stories about the facility being constructed to perform research on genetically modified foods.

The family ran an organic farm, and the older sibling had thought that the genetically modified food experimentation posed a threat to his family's livelihood, and as a result, his inheritance.

The older brother, keen to present a legal and peaceful presence to the outside world had formed The Only Way is Organic as a cover organisation to obtain funds that would ultimately be used by his direct-action group.

The names associated with the peaceful group via its website were people who genuinely supported that group, and as a result, gave their time and money to the cause. They had no idea that the site resided on the same server as an anarchist group, and they definitely didn't have a clue as to the activities of the supposed peace-loving founder of The Only Way is Organic.

After the younger brother caved, the older brother initially denied that he was involved in anything. However, given that both siblings lived with their parents, the parents gave the police permission to search the home for evidence, before both brothers had a chance to destroy anything. In the older brother's room, they found tins of red paint and paint stripper, as well as a digital camera, the serial number matching the one I found in the EXIF data of the crime scene photos. That, my friends, is the legal definition of game, set and match.

The older brother was charged and was awaiting trial on several counts. The younger brother was severely punished. Eventually his brother did the right thing and admitted that he had coerced his younger brother into creating the website, and sending threatening emails.

The younger brother had shown a tremendous amount of technical skill for someone so young; however, he'd made some slip ups, which led me to them.

Ultimately it was the actions of Rebecca Shaw that closed the net on these two brothers. I still can't officially condone what she did, of course. Unofficially, I'll just say, sometimes it's good to fight back. In this case, it stopped more people getting hurt, more property being damaged and two young boys getting deeper into a world of anarchism that might otherwise have engulfed their whole lives.

Ghost Resource

Ghost Resource: Chapter One

You can't polish a turd. This has never been more apparent to me than when I'm leaving the country through Heathrow terminal five, just as I was doing today. I'd just about managed to survive the horrific sweep across the M25 to the terminal five spur road, and was in sight of the futuristic and welcoming looking terminal building.

Okay, I'll admit, it's nicer than any other terminal at Heathrow, but that's like saying that losing your left hand is nicer than losing your right hand if you're right handed. It's a bit less horrific, but still something you really really want to avoid.

I parked at the business class car park and headed to my personal 'shuttle-bubble' thingy which would glide me to the terminal building. A perk of being able to bill travel expenses back to my client, slightly more convenient parking. On the trouble-free ride to the terminal I took in my last doses of 'polish', for I knew that in mere minutes I'd be in the thick of the turd that was the typical Heathrow experience.

Sure enough, I was soon standing at the end of a thirty-minute check-in line, waiting my turn to partake in an unwanted interaction with a bored and depressed looking member of airline staff. She appeared to hate me for the sole reason of wanting to make use of her company's product.

We'd probably get on socially, because as it turned out, I also hated myself for wanting to make use of her company's product. However, duty called, and this time duty was at the end of a fourteen-hour flight to Singapore.

After a few hours milling about the airport, I boarded my flight and was on my way with only the expected half hour Heathrow delay. After the first meal service was done, I pulled out my laptop and began to review the notes I'd made following a phone conversation the previous evening.

I was flying to the Singaporean offices of a UK headquartered semiconductor manufacturing company named PGT Semiconductor. These offices served as the regional headquarters for the company's Asian and Australian operations. I would be arriving on Tuesday morning local time, and making my way directly to a meeting with the leaders of both Human Resources and Finance within that region.

David Oluwafemi was the Head of Finance, and was the person I'd had an hour-long discussion with previously. He was relatively new to the company, which employed around thirty thousand people worldwide.

David had initially spoken with PGT's head of security, a lady named Edith Izzy, who was based in the UK, and was someone I'd done business with previously. David and Edith had discussed a troubling irregularity David had discovered while reviewing invoices submitted by another PGT employee. This lead Edith to call me, and request that I promptly get my arse on a plane to Singapore. Both Edith and David suspected that something fraudulent was occurring, and fearing some internal politics, wanted me to serve as an independent third party to investigate and get to the bottom of what was occurring. It was one of those scenarios that could be nothing, or could be something, but David and Edith wisely wanted to have everything in place before they opened a can of worms.

What I knew so far was that David was familiarizing himself with the accounting software used by PGT, when he stumbled across an invoice submitted by a member of the talent acquisition team based in Singapore. The invoice immediately caught his eye. It was submitted on behalf of a local headhunting company, who were seeking remittance for services rendered. Specifically, executive search services for a new PGT employee. PGT frequently used such companies, so nothing was overly suspicious or unexpected about this. Likewise, I understood it was not unusual for that member of the recruiting team to be the one submitting invoices of this nature.

What was odd about the invoice, was that the new PGT employee that the executive search company were claiming to have helped in the acquisition of, was one Mr. David Oluwafemi, the very same man who was now reviewing said invoice. The problem, David was in fact referred to PGT by another employee, so he knew for certain that no executive search firms had been involved in his hire.

This clearly didn't sit well with him, and he, along with Edith Izzy and the head of HR wanted an explanation

Comfortable that I'd reviewed all of the information received to date, I settled into my seat, took a sip of red wine and sat back to watch the latest terrible Adam Sandler film. Only twelve more hours to go.

My arrival at Changi airport was uneventful and efficient, and lead me to conclude that Heathrow airport management should make the trip over here just to observe how to do things properly. Immigration had been a breeze, and less than half an hour after landing, I was getting into the back of a car that would take me to the PGT offices. I'd never been to Singapore before, but it had been a place I'd wanted to visit for some time. I was a regular television viewer of the Singapore Formula One Grand Prix, which saw cars racing around the very same streets I was now traversing on my ride to the PGT office. Although the actual racing was typically far from the most entertaining, the city never failed to provide a spectacular backdrop for the event. It was just a shame that I'd likely be stuck inside an office that could have been anywhere in the world for the duration of my stay.

Indeed, upon arrival at the office building, I felt a bit short changed given the fact that it was a relatively bland, and short building in a sea of modern, highly reflective skyscrapers. I'd read online that the majority of PGT employees based here were software developers, and many were on contract. It's my experience that software developers, who focus solely on lines of code every day, are typically placed in the less attractive offices, poor folks! I guess the theory is that they have other things to focus on.

I entered the building and began the usual procedure of having my credentials validated by the front desk person. She was a younger lady who was friendly and asked how my flight was, and told me how she wished to visit London one day. I was about to tell her all about the horrors of Heathrow, to try and prevent yet another innocent soul from having to endure its nightmarish lack of organisation, but I stopped myself from doing so. She'd just have to discover it the hard way, like the rest of us did.

I was asked to take a seat and poured myself a drink of lemon infused water from a cooler on the far side of the reception area. In the brief window of time walking to the car from the airport and then again from the car to the office, I'd been exposed to non-air-conditioned air. The result was that Singapore's sticky tropical climate was already making me perspire at an uncomfortable rate.

A tall gentleman wearing a dark suit, shiny red tie, pristine white shirt and blue ID badge on a PGT lanyard hanging around his neck emerged from behind some turnstiles, and headed towards me.

"Parker Foss, David Oluwafemi, a pleasure to meet you", he said as he shook my hand firmly with a vice like grip. "Please, come on back."

David lead me through the same turnstiles from which he had emerged moments earlier, and directed me to his office, which was in the middle of a larger, open plan space. I noted about thirty desks in that particular space, and each one had height adjustable desks and dual monitors on arms. Laptop docking stations were also present, which was of course indicative of a company who supplied their employees with laptops rather than desktops. Not a big thing, but time after time I've found that most 'dodgy' activities that occur on company-owned computer equipment occur on laptops, which can of course be leveraged away from the prying eyes of co-workers. David offered me another drink, this time a cooled bottle of mineral water. I obliged, because I felt that I should take every opportunity to hydrate on this trip. We sat down and began to talk about the investigation that was about to begin.

"Well Parker, as we discussed on the phone, we've got something strange going on in regards to invoices, and we really want to get to the bottom of it." David explained. "In a second, I'll bring in Janis Opal, who is our head of HR out here. Janis will explain to you the main players involved her and where they all fit in."

"Sounds good, I assume that right now no one knows that they're being investigated?" I enquired, while reaching into my bag for my notebook.

"That's correct, we want your opinion on what steps we should take before making the first move here. We really don't want people to get spooked and start destroying potential evidence."

This was a smart and refreshing move, I'd known many investigations go wrong based on an overzealous reaction from the first responders.

I heard a knock on the glass behind me, David beckoned for the person to enter his office. I turned around in my seat to see a tall, dark haired lady in a blue pantsuit. David made the introductions.

"Parker, I'd like to introduce Janis Opal, regional head of HR, Janis, this is Parker Foss, computer investigations wizard."

I stood up and shook Janis's hand. She did not look overly excited to see me. It soon became apparent that her opinion was that human error, rather than fraud was the root cause of the strange invoice.

"I'm sorry that you had to come all the way out here for what will probably turn out to be an innocent mistake Parker, but Edith insisted, and as she is in HQ and well, we really have to follow her wishes," she snapped.

The three of us sat down, and we began to discuss the invoice, a hard copy of which David had in front of him. The printed invoice was turned around so that both myself and Janis could see it.

The invoice had been printed from the accounting software, so included some additional metadata, including the name of the user account used to submit the invoice, and the local time at the time of submission. The submitting account username was 'cathy.leong', and conversation soon turned to the human behind the username.

"Cathy Leong has been with the company around six months, she is a junior member of our talent acquisition team. Her job includes liaising with both third party and internal recruiters. She doesn't do any direct recruiting herself. I've had limited interactions with her, but feedback from her line manager has been positive." Janis paused for a second. "I agree this looks very strange, but I believe that in this instance, there was probably a miscommunication between the search company and herself and somehow the wrong name ended up on the invoice. If I could just talk to her about this, then I could very easily get to the bottom of it."

I could tell from the look on David's face he wasn't so sure. He began to speak while opening his desk drawer and removing a folder.

"Well, we all like to think the best of others, it's human nature, but I'm afraid I've spent some time looking into the a few of the other invoices submitted by Cathy over the last three or four months, and let's just say, if this is a mistake, it appears she makes a lot of mistakes."

David removed a half dozen more invoices and spread them across the table, like a poker player showing his hand.

"Each of these invoices references head hunting services for the named PGT employee. Four of them I've spoken with, and they've confirmed to me that they have never interacted with a head-hunter, they were direct hires. The other two, don't seem to have ever been employees here?! I think she's in cahoots with the head-hunter, and they're charging us for services that we didn't actually receive!"

The revelation visibly caught Janis off guard, and she took more time to ingest the contents of these new invoices.

"Well, I'll agree that this changes things David, let me get Cathy into my office for a chat. I think she's going to have a hard time explaining this, but I want to make sure we discover exactly what is going on. I intend to suspend her during the course of the investigation." Janis said in a somewhat muted tone.

By now it was clear to the three of us that David had uncovered some sort of fraud, but what was not clear was Cathy's exact role, nor how deep into the organization the fraud penetrated.

"Parker, what steps should we take before Janis has the conversation with Cathy?" David enquired.

"Well, let's make sure that the second she enters Janis's office her access to all systems is disabled, and let's seize her company laptop." I instructed. "The objective here is to eliminate the opportunity for her to destroy any evidence."

David and Janis made contact with local IT resources over email and instant message to put together the plan to lock Cathy out of her company owned resources. Based on my observations of the email system in use, I made one further recommendation that I asked to be relayed to IT.

"It looks like you folks are using a Microsoft Exchange server for email. There is a feature in Exchange called 'Litigation Hold' mode, which places a mailbox in a state where even if an item is deleted by a user, it is really still there for the purposes of electronic discovery. I'd suggest placing Cathy's mailbox into litigation hold mode, along with her line manager's and maybe yours too Janis."

The litigation hold was placed, and the arrangements made for Cathy's interview and suspension. The seized laptop would be provided to me for imaging and study.

Both myself and David watched from a distance as a Janis beckoned the fresh faced, smiling Cathy to her office, blissfully unaware that she was about to have a really bad day.

Still, at least her day hadn't begun at Heathrow airport.

Ghost Resource: Chapter Two

David and I watched from a distance, as a visibly tearful Cathy emerged from Janis's private office and was promptly ushered out of the open plan office space. Cathy was not allowed to talk to any of her co-workers, many of whom were staring at her as he was led away.

Another woman got up from the open space and entered Janis's office, the door closed behind them.

"That's Aisha Kadir, Cathy's manager." David explained.

A young man emerged at David's office door with a laptop.

"This is for you, I believe." He said, handing me the powered-on laptop that had been in regular use by Cathy Leong until a few moments ago.

I asked David if I could leverage his office as a makeshift lab for forensically imaging Cathy's laptop. The forensic image created would be a bit by bit copy of the contents of the disk drive, which I could then comb over for clues as to Cathy's involvement with the strange invoices. Given that the laptop was powered on, I'd be performing a 'live' acquisition, which is never your first choice as an investigator but frequently your only option. The best-case scenario is that the machine you need to image is powered off, so that you can physically remove the hard drive and use a piece of hardware called a write blocker to prevent any accidental changes being made to the hard disk under investigation. Any filesystem activity occurring directly on a machine that is being examined has the potential to destroy or invalidate evidence forever, and was to be avoided at all costs if possible. However, when a machine is powered on, powering it off could also cause vital evidence contained in memory or temporary files to be lost. It's a complete catch twenty-two, and one that many investigators have had to face. I had come prepared to take on any kind of acquisition, so this wasn't going to be a problem logistically, I just had to make sure I documented everything that I did with complete accuracy.

Before any imaging began, I took pictures of the laptop and noted the serial number, asset number and model information. I took pictures of the content of the screen. The machine was still logged in as 'Cathy.Leong' and I could see that Microsoft Outlook and Microsoft Word were running. I took pictures of the screen itself, so as to create a record of the state of the machine when it was handed to me. Incidentally, this is the only time in computing that it's okay to use an external camera to take a screenshot, any other time you're being too much of a newb.

It was time to begin the live imaging process. I reached in my bag and pulled out two, one terabyte, external hard drives to use as evidence drives. These drives had been pre-sterilized back in the lab. This meant I'd used a trusted piece of hardware to 'zero-out' the disks, so I could be one hundred percent sure that there was no existing data on them which could contaminate the evidence that I was acquiring from Cathy's laptop.

Secondly, I had a smaller USB drive, which contained the 'lite' version of a piece of software called FTK imager. FTK imager is part of the Forensic Toolkit suite of tools that is used across the world in forensic investigations. FTK Imager is used to collect evidence, which can later be processed in the main FTK software application. The fact that I was using the lite version was significant. This version doesn't require me to install any files locally to my target machine, it runs exclusively in random access memory. This significantly reduces the footprint of the FTK imager application on the computer, and therefore reduces the chances of evidence spoliation occurring.

I inserted my USB drive, and one of the external hard drives. I began the disk imaging process, which would take several minutes to complete. As the imaging progress bar slowly crawled along, Janis Opal, the head of HR, re-entered David's office.

"How did it go?" I asked Janis, hoping for some insight into the meeting she'd just had with Cathy, our person of interest.

"Well, Cathy was very upset, and denied that she was up to anything fraudulent. She said that all of the invoices she submitted were merely forwarded to her from Aisha Kadir, her line manager." Janis explained.

I recalled that I'd seen Aisha Kadir enter Janis's office immediately after Cathy was escorted out. I enquired as to her level of knowledge about the investigation. Given that one of her employees had just been suspended, I figured she'd now be in the loop. I was right.

"I explained the situation to Aisha, and she was shocked." Janis explained. "She says she often forwards invoices to Cathy to be submitted in this way, but she says she's never seen an invoice for search services for David, or any of the other employees that were direct hires. She said there would be no such thing." Janis paused and looked over to where Aisha was sitting. "She actually looked extremely sad. She has been mentoring Cathy since she began working here, and says that she feels betrayed that Cathy would do this, and then try and shift the responsibility onto her."

The imaging of Cathy's machine continued in the background. Reaching for my notebook, I started to write down some key facts. The invoices were all entered into the accounting system by Cathy, this was a fact. Cathy had called this out specifically in her meeting with Janis. If the invoices had been forwarded by Aisha, as Cathy had claimed, there could be evidence of this in email, which if there, would materialise in a couple of places. Firstly, on Cathy's laptop, in the Microsoft Outlook '.ost' or '.pst' files. OST files are used to store a local copy of email that is on an organization's central Microsoft Exchange Server, whereas PST files are used to store mail that is collected from other types of web based account, or as an archive of Exchange emails. Both Outlook file types can be invaluable sources of evidence relating to email. Secondly, there could be evidence on the company's Exchange server itself, although this might take longer to obtain.

The other confirmed fact was that a second person, Aisha, who was potentially also a person of interest within this investigation, was now aware of this investigation. This changed the dynamic slightly.

So far, the only evidence I had linking the suspect invoices to a specific person pointed to Cathy, however, experience has shown me that frequently more than one person is involved when internal fraud is suspected. However, with no evidence against Aisha other than Cathy's word, I knew I'd need to either need to convince Janis that Aisha should be treated as a suspect, or find evidence which backed up Cathy's claim that she was just doing her job submitting invoices forwarded to her by her boss.

Given that the imaging process was still ongoing on Cathy's laptop, I decided to test the water in regards to Aisha's potential involvement.

"Well guys, given that Aisha could also be involved here, can we seize her laptop and restrict her access for the time being?" My question was met with stares and silence. "You know, just until I can find evidence on Cathy's computer, that proves she is the true source of these invoices?"

Janis looked slightly perturbed by my suggestion.

"I don't think that is necessary. Aisha was one of the first employees in this office when we opened, she has a long and successful history with the company. I think we'd be doing her a huge disservice by accusing her of something with only the word of someone who has been with us for all of five minutes against her."

It was clearly a sensitive topic so I didn't want to push Janis much further on the issue right now. It was still going to be a while until I'd be able to run the contents of Cathy's laptop through the FTK case processing engine. This would build a searchable map of her hard drive, including files that had been deleted. I decided that I'd turn my attention to another line of enquiry, while the imaging was ongoing.

"David, can you provide me copies of all those invoices?" I asked. He obliged and headed to a nearby photocopier. My intent was to do some open source intelligence gathering into the headhunting companies that had invoiced PGT for services that seemingly hadn't been rendered. Open source intelligence, or OSINT, is a term for the identification of information about a subject by way of publicly available information, such as public records, search engine results or social media information.

The scent of freshly applied toner wafted in through the door as David returned with two copies of each invoice. He distributed them evenly between myself and Janis. One copy for me and one for her.

I could tell pretty quickly that the invoices appeared to have been prepared by two different vendors. The first, was named 'Lian and Partners'. The second vendor was named 'SingaPro'. I asked Janis if she was familiar with either of the two vendors. She personally hadn't heard of them, but explained that she rarely did any work on recruiting in her current role, so that shouldn't come as a surprise.

"The talent team has a budget, they use it with whichever vendors they see fit," she explained.

The invoice that had started this whole investigation, had been submitted on behalf of Lian and Partners. After a brief logistical exercise, I was able to get my laptop on the office guest Wi-Fi network. I used my new-found access to consult my best friend, Mr. Google.

After trying multiple variations of 'Lian and Partners', 'Singapore' and 'Executive Search' it became clear that either the company didn't exist, or had absolutely zero web presence. This was highly suspect. Looking for other information on the invoices, I noted a bank account number and the name of the person who had signed the invoice, a Mr. Matt Phua.

I turned to the tool that has emerged as a strong contender for the title of most useful, cost effective, investigative tool of the decade. Facebook.com.

I'm a Facebook user myself, but you'll never catch me using my actual account during an investigation. I'm far too paranoid that I'll accidentally add the person I'm investigating as a friend, and that'd be rather embarrassing. It almost happened once while I was digging around looking for password ideas to get access to an encrypted partition I'd discovered on a client's laptop. It's amazing how many people still set their password to be their kids or pets names, all perfectly available information on Facebook, with a poor privacy configuration. I logged into Facebook with one of my many 'fake' accounts, reserved for just this purpose.

I ran a search for Matt Phua on Facebook. There were of course many hits, so I decided to try something a little different. I ran a search for Cathy Leong. I wanted to see if the Cathy Leong we were investigating had an account on Facebook, and if she did, did she have any friends named Matt Phua. I found an account with a profile picture that looked a lot like our Cathy, but given that I'd only seen her from a distance, I asked Janis to verify.

"Yes, that's her, but I must say, I don't know how comfortable I am with you digging around our employees personal Facebook profiles," she exclaimed. It wasn't the first time I'd heard such objections, but thankfully I had a stock answer ready to roll.

"Facebook is a treasure trove of intelligence; people have the choice to limit public access to their profiles. If the choose not to, then the information they put out there is a matter of public record, and folks like me can exploit it as such."

Janis, clearly unimpressed with my answer, decided it was time for her to leave, and do some other work.

"David, ping me if you discover any further information. I've cleared my calendar, so will be available if you need me," she said on her way out of the office.

Turning my attention back to Cathy's Facebook page, I decided to study her list of friends. My working theory was that maybe Cathy was working with an associate, who had established a headhunting company. I searched the name Matt Phua. Low and behold I got a hit. Cathy had a Facebook friend called Matthew Phua, who according to his profile, was located in Singapore. An interesting development, I'm sure you'll agree, but I always like to give people the benefit of the doubt. Perhaps she met him through the search company, and they'd become friends? Perhaps it was a completely different person with the same name. My earlier search had shown how common the name was. In any case, I entered the development into my notebook.

I examined Matthew Phua's profile, looking for information that might link him to Lian and Partners. There was nothing. He listed his occupation as an IT consultant at a local company.

'Matt Phua' was the signatory on all of the remaining Lian and Partners invoices. I turned my attention to the SingaPro invoices.

A Google search for 'SingaPro' yielded much the same results as my previous searches. A whole load of nothing. Either these search companies didn't really need a web presence, or they weren't real entities. Indeed, I happened to note that the SingaPro invoices contained a detail missing from those of Lian and Partners, a contact email address. An email address would typically serve to enhance the credibility of a company, but in this case, that email address was a free 'Gmail' account. Now, I get that some businesses use free email accounts, but typically those companies are Gardeners or Hair Stylists, not recruiters who seek to hire executives and high tech talent. Why anyone would see that on an invoice and not get suspicious, was mind boggling to me.

There was a name for the signatory on the invoice, Kelly Lim. I quickly searched for Kelly Lim amongst Cathy's Facebook friends. This time there was no match.

A global search for Kelly Lim on Facebook revealed multiple hits, far too many to spend time looking at. This was something I'd have to revisit later, as there was little point chasing down individuals on invoices that displayed signs of fraud when I hadn't yet validated that the companies who supposedly produced them were even real.

I needed to determine if both Lian and Partners, and SingaPro were actually registered entities in Singapore.

A little online research pointed me in the direction of Bizfile, an online portal that allowed a person to register a company with the Government of Singapore. Much like 'Companies House' does in the UK, it was also possible to search for records relating to a business, including the registered Director and Secretary.

Using the portal, I ran a search for Lian and Partners. I was actually pretty surprised to see a result. A company with that name was formed some five months earlier. I clicked for more information, I wanted to see the names of the people who had registered Lian and Partners. I waited with bated breath for the page to slowly load.

"Director and Secretary information is available, for the fee of $15 SGP," the screen read.

Ugh. How frustrating. I reached into my pocket for my wallet. It was of course very worth the small charge to reveal the secrets of Lian and Partners, but it was still a frustrating roadblock to have to pay for public information. The charge paid, I was sent a link with access to the record I had requested. Again, the page took forever to load, but when it did, it delivered. I beckoned David over. I read the text on the screen aloud to him.

"Lian and Partners, registered Director, Ms. C Leong."

"Well, there you go," said David. "She registered her own company, and then invoiced us for their services, and she did it multiple times!" David upped and left to go get Janis.

I sat back in my chair to take it all in. I appeared to have just solved in case in less time than it took me to travel to client location, and I'd done it using open source information. Things really didn't look good for Cathy, as far as her innocence, but I still wanted to disprove her claim that the invoices had been forwarded to her by Aisha, her manager, before I called this one case closed.

With David still out of the room, I returned to the Bizfile portal and repeated the entity search and payment procedure, this time for SingaPro. The company had been registered about three weeks before Lian and Partners. Sure enough, Ms. C Leong was listed as a registered Director once again.

I heard a tone from my FTK imager session. My image was complete, and I had an FTK case to build.

Ghost Resource: Chapter Three

I made the decision to head to my hotel to work on the image of Cathy's laptop. The discovery of Cathy's name on the company registration documents had caused quite the stir back at the PGT office, and preparations were already underway to have her fired, and for local law enforcement to become involved. The finance team had begun a full audit of all the invoices she'd ever submitted for payment.

Cathy's actual laptop had been locked away in a safe in the office, to which only the front desk security person had access. Chain of custody forms had been completed, so that we had a paper trail to back up the laptop's movements.

I began to comb through the contents of Cathy's laptop. Rather than blindly searching, I had a hit list of things I was going to target.

First on the Agenda, I wanted to disprove the allegation that Aisha had forwarded Cathy the invoices from Lian and Partners and SingaPro via email. To do this in FTK was very simple. The product automatically discovers and indexes all emails from Outlook, and sorts them in a variety of different ways, such as by date, or by sender. This included both emails that were still actively in the mailbox, as well as deleted items.

One thing became apparent, Cathy kept a clean mailbox. She had only twelve messages in her inbox, and a around two dozen more in carefully organized folders. Her deleted items contained only a handful of messages too, meaning she frequently cleaned those up as well. People like this frustrate me, not only are they hard to investigate, but they also make me feel bad about my own email hygiene.

Of all the emails, around ten of them came from Aisha, all were work related and routine, and none of them mentioned any of the vendors that I was interested in. This was one of those rare instances where email had been a dead end, and importantly, didn't back up Cathy's claim that she'd received the invoices from Aisha.

It was time to try a different approach, a keyword search. FTK allows me to search across the entire contents of a hard drive for a keyword, or combination of keywords. I kicked off a search for the keywords 'Lian AND Partners'. Zero results. How about just 'Lian'? There were a handful of results, but none of them were relevant. Next I tried 'SingaPro', and there was a hit. Interestingly, it was in the body of an instant message conversation, between Cathy and Aisha. My heart started to beat faster.

PGT was using Microsoft Lync to communicate internally, and in most deployments, Lync was configured to store conversation histories. Few people realise this, and I'd found plenty of evidence in stored Lync conversations before.

This conversation appeared to be a routine exchange between Cathy and Aisha that had occurred around three months prior.

"Hey Cat, did you upload all those invoices I gave you yesterday?" Aisha asked. The response from Cathy, came around a minute later.

"Yes, PPT, Apex and SingaPro, all uploaded yesterday."

"Ok. Great, thanks! :-)" Aisha acknowledged.

This Lync exchange was extremely interesting. Why would Cathy willingly disclose that she had uploaded an invoice from a company that she had registered in her own name to her manager? Why would her manager not question the name of the vendor if she hadn't forwarded it on? Things just got more complex.

Aisha, either through an oversight or malice had now re-entered the scope of the investigation. I felt like this little Lync message gave me enough to justify going back to Janis Opal and asking for Aisha's laptop for investigation.

I called David and explained my finding. He agreed that it was unusual, and promised to work on getting Janis to agree to seizing the laptop and having it sent to me at the hotel. He told me to expect a call from him in an hour.

In the meantime, I went back to working on the laptop image and my hit list of items. If Cathy was creating these invoices as well as submitting them, there was a chance that she was doing it on her laptop, and I wanted to look for evidence of that. I looked through documents, spreadsheets and image files. Nothing of value was found. There was no evidence that any of the invoices were created on her machine. This either meant she was smart enough not to create them on her work computer, which was entirely possible, or that she hadn't created them in the first place.

I decided to run a few of the names that I'd stumbled across during the course of my investigation through the keyword search. First I tried Matt Phua, the name from the Lian and Partners invoice. There were hits in the temporary internet files. It appeared Cathy had visited Matt Phua's Facebook profile a couple of times. I flicked the various hits, until I found something interesting in the page file. The page file, on a Windows system, is a portion of the computer's hard drive that is used as if it were RAM. Temporary content is written to the page file by any application that is running, this includes web browsers. In this case, the keyword search for Matt Phua had hit upon a conversation taking place via the Facebook messaging platform that had found its way into the often-juicy content of the page file. I examined the content of the hit and was able to dissect the conversation.

"Yo Matt, by any chance are you working for a headhunting company now?"

"Lol no, still in IT! Why? How's your sister?"

"Ha, I got an invoice from a company we work with and it was signed by someone with the same name as you. Thought you might have given up being a nerd. She's good, still single! ;-)"

Clearly, the conversation appeared to be between Cathy and her Facebook friend, Matt Phua. It also might have just been the most important conversation she'd ever had on Facebook, because it appeared to once again exonerate her from any insider knowledge of the company that was registered in her name.

How quickly things change in investigations, just a few hours earlier, it looked as if Cathy was done for. Now, I had my doubts.

The phone rang, it was David.

"Parker, Aisha's laptop is on its way over to you. We told her that we were looking for information from Cathy, and she was happy to hand it over. One of my employees will be at your hotel within the next few minutes, and don't worry I filled out one of those chain of custody forms you left behind."

This was great news, but I was extremely mindful of the time window between Aisha becoming aware of the investigation into Cathy, and losing access to her laptop. There would have been plenty of time for her to destroy or damage evidence that might link her to the invoices.

Then, I had a brainwave. While Aisha would have had the opportunity to alter the contents of her laptop, she would have not been afforded that luxury with her Microsoft Exchange account, which had been placed in Litigation Hold mode at my request earlier. Even if she deleted items, they wouldn't really be deleted, given the mode her mailbox was in.

I made a frantic call to David, and asked if he could arrange with IT for a PST copy of the mailbox to be sent to me via a secure file transfer service I subscribed too. I hadn't been able to find evidence of Aisha sending the invoices in the cleanliness of Cathy's mailbox, but maybe coming at it from the other side would warrant better results.

The wheels were placed in motion on my request for the PST file, and in the meantime, I headed down to the lobby where I met a PGT employee who handed over Aisha's laptop. The employee was a younger gentleman. I didn't catch his name. We completed the chain of custody documentation and said our goodbyes.

I headed back up to my room and began imaging Aisha's laptop. This machine was powered down, so a routine offline acquisition was called for. I carefully unscrewed the hard disk from the machine and attached it to a write blocker. I imaged the machine to my other evidence drive.

While that process was ongoing, I received notification that I'd received the PST file of Aisha's mailbox from PGT's IT staff. I promptly downloaded the file and added it to my FTK case. After a few minutes of indexing, I was ready to examine the contents of Aisha's mailbox.

It soon became apparent that Aisha was also big into mailbox cleanliness, as very few emails existed in her inbox or sent items. It was also apparent that she'd very recently picked up this habit. Extremely recently in fact, like, within the last two hours!

The evidence showed that Aisha had deleted a few thousand emails that morning, pretty much the entire contents of her mailbox. However, because the litigation hold flag had been set, as far as the Exchange server was concerned, this had no impact whatsoever. Asking for that to be switched on was a good call methinks.

So, the question now, was why had Aisha attempted to delete her emails? What was in there that she was trying to bury? The answer was easily discovered in FTK.

I sorted email by recipient, and looked for messages she'd sent to Cathy. There were lots, and many of them contained invoices. I desperately tabbed through the search results. I wanted to uncover one of those golden invoices that David had identified as fraudulent. Bingo! I found the one with David's name on, attached to an email sent to Cathy, with a subject of 'upload please' and no message in the body of the email. No wonder Aisha had tried to cover this up, this was pretty damming.

Now I'd found evidence that had shown very clearly Aisha was in on things, but I hadn't found any evidence that Cathy was not involved. Indeed, the company registration in Cathy's name was still the most significant piece of evidence against her. Although the Facebook conversation with her friend Matt was still something of an abnormality.

It was getting late in the day, so I wanted to get one final call in to David and Janis. They needed to know about the discovery indicating Aisha's involvement, and would have to make a decision about what to do with her during the remainder of the investigation.

Janis was understandably taken aback when presented with the evidence that the invoices had in fact been forwarded by Aisha, and that she'd blatantly attempted to hide that fact.

"Well Parker, I just don't know what to say. Aisha has left for the day, but I'll call her early tomorrow and I guess we'll place her on suspension until we figure this whole thing out. It certainly sounds like there was involvement from both parties."

I ended my call and returned to FTK, the imaging of Aisha's laptop had completed. It was time to add the image to FTK case, and see what clues could be found on the laptop.

While everything was processing, I decided to flop down on the king bed behind me. I'd been feeling the jet lag slowly creeping in over the last hour, and now it was time to surrender to it. My eyes began to close and I feel into a rewarding slumber.

Ghost Resource: Chapter Four

I looked over at the red LCD display of the hotel room alarm clock, it was four thirty AM, and my confused body clock was telling me it was time to wake up. I didn't mind, because I glanced at the screen of my FTK session which informed me that my evidence, Aisha's laptop hard drive, had finished processing and was ready for me to get stuck into.

The first thing I looked at was email. I wanted to compare and contrast the locally held emails with those I'd identified on the Exchange server previously. As expected, Aisha had been on a deleting spree, and the laptop wasn't going to give up any more information in email than I had already obtained from Exchange.

I wanted to review all lines of communication between Aisha and Cathy that I could find. If they were in fact colluding, there might very well be evidence of that on this laptop. I read through pages of IM messages between the two of them, and other than the mention of SingaPro, which I'd already seen from the other side. There was very little chatter about invoices, and definitely nothing that stuck out.

I did a keyword search for 'Cathy', and my attention was drawn to a file that FTK noted had been deleted from Aisha's desktop. It was a simple text file, containing Cathy's full name and what appeared to be an address and date of birth. I noted that it interesting that a manager would have this information on their machine, but not incriminating in anyway. This particular search revealed nothing further of interest, so I moved on.

Repeating the steps, I'd taken on Cathy's laptop, I ran a search for 'Lian and Partners'. Unlike Cathy's machine, a deleted Word document which appeared to be the source file for one of the invoices appeared. This was golden. David had confirmed to me earlier that the invoices were uploaded to the accounting system as PDF's. I just found a trace of the original document that had been used to create that PDF, and I'd found it on Aisha's work machine. This was brazen.

This discovery further solidified Aisha's involvement. She was clearly the one making some of the invoices, even if she wasn't smart enough to do so on another computer.

Perhaps Cathy was also making invoices, but on another machine? Who was the mastermind? How many other people were involved? These were all questions I knew that PGT would want answered, and I'd have to keep digging to find an answer.

I paused to shower and run down to get a quick breakfast from the hotel restaurant. The rumbling of my stomach had become too much of a distraction, not to mention I was still grimy feeling from having travelled here the day before.

I secured all evidence and systems in my hotel safety deposit box and left the room. I noticed a piece of paper had been jammed in the door. Removing the paper, I read the handwritten content.

"Aisha Kadir has been investigated before. Cathy didn't do anything. Please, you must prove this."

I've been doing this type of work for a while, and I can honestly say that I've never had anyone track me down a shove a note in my door, protesting the innocence of someone who was under investigation. Intrigued, and somewhat freaked out, I looked around before continuing my journey to the restaurant. There was no one in sight.

I was eating breakfast when my phone rang. It was a Facetime call from David at PGT. He wanted an update on any additional findings I had made. I briefed him on the documents I'd discovered, that were likely the source of the invoices.

"This is a fascinating discovery, Parker. Here we're still working on the assumption that both Cathy and the Aisha are involved," David explained. "Janis Opal actually took a call from Cathy last night, she wanted to know more about why she was suspended. We let her know about the company registrations in her name. She claimed that she'd never registered a company, didn't even know how too, and denied any involvement. She was very upset. Once again, she claims to have just been following instructions from Aisha, in regards to processing the invoices."

I decided to tell David about the note I'd received in my hotel room. I explained that the note claimed Cathy's innocence, and eluded to the fact that Aisha had been investigated before.

"I can't answer on Aisha," he explained. "I'll have to have Janis discuss that with you, but, one thing I can say for sure is that I've had more than a couple of people mention to me how highly they think of Cathy."

Comparing how both and Aisha and Cathy had responded to the investigation unfolding around them, Cathy did seem the more innocent. Then again, it was going to be very hard for Cathy to shake that black mark of being the person who appeared on the company registration documents.

I ended my phone call with David, and headed back to my hotel room. I unpacked my laptop from the safe and prepared to get stuck back into the investigation.

I'd been interrupted by my hunger previously, so I needed to review my notes to determine exactly where I'd gotten to in the investigative flow.

SingaPro was at the top of my list, and that was my next keyword search term. I wanted to see if there were any hits on that search term in Aisha's laptop.

The search revealed about a half dozen results. Not in any documents or emails, but instead within a file called 'formhistory.sqlite'. I recognized this file, it was a SQLite database file that was used by the Mozilla Firefox web browser to store previously entered values in web forms. You know, if you enter a bunch of data in a form, the browser saves it so if you revisit that form, the entries can auto-populate. This discovery could simply indicate that Aisha performed a web search for the term 'SingaPro' but it was hard to tell looking at it in FTK. I needed to use a more specialized tool to review the structure of the SQLite file. Fortunately, I had one, an open source tool called DB Browser for SQLite. DB Browser for SQLite allowed me to open a SQLite format file and review the tables it contained in a more natural format. I used the export function in FTK to grab the SQLite file, and opened it in the DB Browser application.

Examining the table in the SQLite file I reviewed the names of the columns. I'd worked with this type of file before, but it was still worth the time to re-familiarise myself with the structure. 'Fieldname', 'value', 'first_used' and 'times_used' were the column names. The names were pretty self-explanatory. The fieldname and value columns were used to store the mapping of form field ID's with the value that had been added to them. If you view the HTTP source code behind any html form, you'll see the 'id' parameter that is used to give the field a unique identifier. This same ID was the one that ended up in Firefox's 'formhistory.sqlite' database, in the 'fieldname' column.

In the case of Aisha's machine, I'd been led to the SQLite database by the term, 'SingaPro' which was in the value column. Studying the field name associated with that value, I could see it had been submitted in a field called 'bizfile_register_entity_name'. Bizfile?! That was the same government portal I'd used to search for company information yesterday? Register_Entity_Name?! On my laptop, I browsed back to bizfile site, and viewed the HTML source of the page. Every form field id value began with 'bizfile_'. Holy smokes! Had I just discovered that the Firefox browser on Aisha's machine was used to register the company SingaPro, through the Bizfile portal? It certainly looked that way, but I wanted more information to be sure.

I continued to study the structure of the SQLite file, looking for evidence to support that hypothesis. Other fieldnames included 'Register_Director_Last' which had a value of 'Leong'. 'Register_Director_Address' which had a value matching the address that I'd noted earlier in the deleted text file on Aisha's desktop.

It was now looking pretty certain that this machine was used to register those companies, which was clearly a very significant finding. The 'formhistory.sqlite' file was found under Aisha's user profile, so I could also be certain that the machine was logged in under her account when that action was completed.

I wrote up the finding and headed down to the hotel lobby. I planned to head into the office to present my discovery to David and Janis.

I jumped in a taxi and sat back, pondering this latest twist. It now looked to me as if Aisha had registered the company in Cathy's name. This would be consistent with the other evidence. Cathy's Facebook conversation with Matt Phua, the forwarded but deleted emails in Aisha's mailbox, the instant message conversation between Cathy and Aisha.

I arrived at the PGT office, and was promptly greeted by David.

"David, have I got some news for you!" I exclaimed. "I think I've found the smoking gun, I found evidence that Aisha's laptop was the one used to register at least one of those companies in Cathy's name!" I expected David to react positively. Instead, he barely reacted at all.

"Well, Parker, step into my office, and we can chat about that some more," he said.

We entered David's office where Janis Opal was also waiting, Janis shut the door behind me. I could sense something wasn't right.

"Parker, I, we, just got a call from Cathy Leong's brother.." Janis paused for a second, apparently to compose herself. "Unfortunately, Cathy took her own life this morning."

Talk about hearing something completely unexpected. In all my years, I'd never experienced such a gut wrenching feeling as I did in that second. I felt like I'd be hit by a freight train.

"Good lord." I said, slowly lowering myself into a chair. "That is horrible."

I didn't know Cathy of course, I'd never interacted with her. I'd only seen her briefly as she was lead out of the office yesterday, but that didn't stop the wave of grief that I felt.

"There was a note, apparently," David interjected. "She said she was innocent and was being set up, but didn't think anyone would believe her and didn't want to go to jail."

The three of us sat in silence for a while.

"That poor girl, if she'd have waited, I mean, I've found the evidence that bloody well exonerates her."

I gave a summary of the finding I'd recently made in the Firefox SQLite database, to Janis and David. They both agreed, that it definitely placed the guilt with Aisha. Not that it really mattered anymore.

"I recently found out that Aisha was investigated for suspected fraud once before. Nothing like this, and nothing was ever proven," Janis explained. "I just wish I knew this sooner; it could have prevented all of this from happening. After all, where there's smoke, there's fire."

What had started out as a fairly straightforward corporate fraud investigation with one suspect, had become a back and forth between two suspects, before finally the digital evidence eliminated one suspect from the case all together. Unfortunately, that same suspect had eliminated herself in the most drastic way possible, and didn't allow enough time for the evidence to save her.

Rarely in this profession do we see so powerfully the effect on real lives that digital evidence can have.

I wrote up my final reports and findings for David and Janis and headed for Changi airport. I'd done my part, and they intended to work with local law enforcement to prosecute Aisha.

I just needed to get out of there. A fourteen-hour flight followed, and I didn't sleep a wink.

Ghost Resource: Epilogue

A week or so later, I met Edith Izzy, PGT's head of security in a London bar for a debrief session.

Edith filled me in on how the investigation had panned out. In total, $100,000 SGP worth of invoices submitted by Aisha over the preceding six months had been determined to be fraudulent.

Aisha had been suspended and all evidence had been handed over to the local police force. The police had enough evidence to arrest Aisha, but there was one slight problem, they sat on it for a little bit too long.

Once I'd returned to the UK, I'd received a request for some follow up work from Janis Opal. I was asked to search Aisha's laptop once again, this time I was tasked with looking for documents that might indicate Aisha's future plans.

I'd discovered documents relating to Australian immigration, that were filled out with information regarding Aisha and her family members. When the police arrived, Aisha and her family had gone. Presumably headed down under to start a new life. Time will tell if the law ever catches up with her.

Of course, one person who certainly wouldn't be starting a new life, was poor Cathy Leong, who'd tragically lost hers, effectively at the hands of Aisha Kadir, who had planned on framing her all along.

Too distraught at the thought of losing her freedoms and reputation. The idea of being made to pay for a crime she didn't commit, she decided to take the only way out she could see.

Her family, friends and co-workers mourned her.

I thought about her a lot as well. Sometimes I found myself questioning if I could have searched faster. If I should have pushed Janis harder for access to Aisha's laptop.

Ultimately, I became content, and knew that I'd done the best I could, but it was certainly a sobering experience.

It made me realise, more than ever, that when I'm rummaging around in data, it's not just a collection of zeros and ones. It represents people's lives and livelihoods.

In a way, Cathy's death gave me a renewed drive, a renewed determination to make sure that I'd always get to the bottom of any cybercrime investigation. To ensure that people like her, who would become victims of crimes committed in the murky digital landscape, could be saved.

Revenge on the Wire

Revenge on the Wire: Chapter One

My local gym was designed by someone with a sick mind. I know this because they put the changing rooms at the bottom of a significant flight of stairs, which I was now faced with climbing. Typically, that'd be fine, but I'd just finished my first workout in over a week, and my legs were toast.

I tried to work out most days, but the last week had been crazy. I'd had meetings or phone calls with numerous clients who needed computer security incident response help.

The sudden spike in incidents at multiple clients was not some strange coincidence. Businesses all over the globe were assessing the impact of a major security vulnerability that had been discovered in a commonly used internet protocol, Secure Sockets Layer.

The vulnerability, which had gone undiscovered for almost two years, was causing all kinds of information security nightmares. It placed passwords and other sensitive information transmitted across the Internet at risk. Typically, software vulnerabilities are identified by a series of numbers. This was such a significant vulnerability, it had been given a proper name, Heartbleed. As a result of the significant press around Heartbleed, many organisations, including a number of my clients apparently, were assuming that each and every abnormality they saw in their infrastructure was related to the vulnerability. It turned out that each case I'd worked on so far as a direct result of the Heartbleed hype had been a false positive. An event explainable by something completely unrelated and non-malicious, just something that hadn't been noticed before.

Begrudgingly, I put my right foot on the bottom step of the gym stairwell, it was time to get this final few seconds of leg punishment out of the way for the day. I felt the burn in my calf as I began to shift my weight, but the sensation was soon blocked by another. My phone was vibrating in my pocket. I didn't care who was on the end of the line, it could have been a scam artist telling me I'd won a cruise, or an elderly relative I'd purposefully not spoken to for three years. Whomever it was, they were in for a long conversation, because little did they know, they'd given me a great excuse to postpone my ascent into the thumping techno music on the main floor of the gym above.

"Hello, is this Parker Foss?" the muted voice on the end of the line asked.

"Yes, this is Parker, how can I help you?" I responded, double checking the number on the screen, it wasn't one I recognized.

"Parker, how soon can you be in Slough?"

As it happened, I could be in Slough in a couple of hours, provided I left my base in the Cotswolds within a few minutes. Now, had the question been, do I want to be in Slough? The answer would have been a resounding no, because of course, no one ever wants to go to Slough.

After pressing the caller for more information as to why my presence was desired in the fair town of Slough, I was both intrigued, and happy to pick up a new customer. I took a deep breath, and began the painful ascent of the stairs.

I made a quick pit stop at my lab to grab some equipment, and the local sandwich place for a BLT before heading on my way.

The office I was visiting was perched on the edge of the infamous Slough Trading Estate which was home to hundreds of businesses. I located my destination and then encountered a new challenge, finding somewhere to park.

I saw traffic wardens circling like frenzied sharks, and was determined not to become the latest unintentional donor to the coffers of Slough Borough council.

After a fifteen-minute delay while waiting for someone to back an oversized four-by-four out of a space onto a busy street, I finally entered the building.

I was in the headquarters of Remoteli, a tech company providing outsourced, or "managed" in their words, helpdesk services for a varied client base. This was a relatively small office space, occupying only half of a floor of the five-story building, so I figured there couldn't be more than about twenty people working there.

After exchanging pleasantries with the receptionist, I was taken back to meet with Remoteli's Chief Financial Officer, Sarah Williams. On my way to Sarah's office, I studied the lay of the land.

The space, although small, was tricked out like any Silicon Valley start-up. There was a gaming area, thought pods, beer and cider on tap. All that was missing was the Silicon Valley weather. This was Berkshire, not the bay area.

Most of the folks were in open-plan desk rows, however Sarah had a dedicated office with a sliding glass door, a pretty smart idea for someone on the phone talking sensitive financial matters all day. Sarah had been the voice at the other end of the phone call beckoning me to Slough.

After five minutes of what I like to call 'the NDA shuffle', where I am made to agree not to talk about what I'm about to hear, I was more than ready to find out about my latest mission. Safe in the knowledge that the legal stuff was sorted, Sarah began to open up about the reason her company needed my assistance.

"It's been a strange few days for us, Parker. It all started on Tuesday, one of our biggest clients experienced significant disruption, which ultimately, they've attributed to an error by us. However, our internal investigation has failed to provide a decent explanation," Sarah explained, turning her laptop to face me as she did.

"This is a screenshot from one workstation impacted by this event."

The screenshot showed a login screen on a workstation owned by one of Remoteli's customers, with what appeared to be a pretty innocuous error message – 'your password has expired'.

The problem, Sarah explained, was that every password at the company, a pharmaceutical company employing five-thousand people, had expired at the same time. This included all of the system administrators. The customer had been paralysed for hours while the issues were resolved. Remoteli was facing a significant bill, plus the prospect of losing the customer forever.

"Our initial thought was a mistake by one of our employees lead to this event, but no one has admitted resetting all those passwords. Even accidentally," Sarah turned her laptop back towards herself.

"Well, one thing I can understand is that people might be nervous to admit the mistake, especially considering the impact of such a mistake," I responded. "One thing I can't understand is why you wouldn't be able to make the determination as to who made the mistake by reviewing log files. You do have logs, right?" I asked, praying internally that they did have some sort of audit trail.

"Unfortunately, we don't," Sarah responded, once again turning her laptop back towards me, this time more rapidly, as if to literally use it to deflect from my last question. "And that's not everything, just yesterday something else strange happened. We're going through our end of year annual review process right now. All pay increases and bonus requests were suddenly rejected in our HRIS system, apparently by our CEO. Although, as you'd expect, he didn't actually do it," Sarah explained, showing me another screenshot, this time of an automated email.

Remoteli was using a cloud based HRIS product, Readiwork. HRIS systems are used to track everything about an employee, including payments made to the employee, performance reviews and holiday time taken.

The email included in the screenshot read 'Philip Francis has rejected the merit increase for Rebecca Forsythe'. That email also included a section for custom text. While reading the custom text, my heart skipped a beat. I read it aloud in disbelief. "Sorry Rebecca, my heartbleeds for you."

In my mind, this absolutely had to be a reference to the mega-vulnerability that was currently the hot topic amongst the information security community.

Was a system at Remoteli vulnerable to Heartbleed? And was that system used as a vector to obtain access to Remoteli credentials? These were all questions running through my mind. Perhaps finally, I'd been brought into an actual Heartbleed related compromise? It certainly looked that way.

I asked Sarah if she was aware of the Heartbleed vulnerability.

"Well I saw something on the news about a bad virus last night, but that's about it," she responded.

Resisting the urge to go down the road of pedantically explaining the difference between a vulnerability and virus, as I had done about fifty million times in my career, I gently explained what Heartbleed was all about.

"Heartbleed is a vulnerability in an implementation of Secure Sockets Layer, the protocol used to encrypt web traffic. It is possible to steal sensitive information leveraging the Heartbleed vulnerability, if you find a machine susceptible to it. This includes clear text credentials," I explained.

"Do you know, or would anyone else here know if your systems have been checked for the Heartbleed vulnerability, and if so, have they been patched?"

"I will introduce you to Adam Kennedy, our IT guy. He'll be the one to answer that question. Adam is actually a contractor who works for a few companies in the area, so I'll see if he can swing by if he isn't here," Sarah said, while scrolling through the contacts in her phone.

I reflected on two small yet important details that had been conveyed in the conversation with Sarah to this point. Remoteli was a tech company without a dedicated IT person, and clearly didn't have sufficient logging available. If they did, it could have made this investigation a breeze. Given this, it wouldn't have been unreasonable to assume that server patching was also lacking. I'd reserve final judgement until I'd spoken to Adam Kennedy.

"Hi Adam," Sarah spoke into her phone while opening and closing her sliding glass door, she continued the rest of the conversation on the other side of the sliding glass. As a result, the rest of the conversation was muffled, but it seemed as if Sarah was getting into a somewhat heated exchange with Adam. The conversation ended and Sarah popped her head back through the door.

"Sorry about that, discussing whether this was scheduled or emergency time. Typical contractor! He'll be here in half an hour. Would you like a cup of tea?"

"Oh, I'd love one. Thank you."

Sarah beckoned me out of the office and into a kitchenette area. There was momentary mild panic as it appeared the only tea bags left were of the fruity or green variety. Thankfully, a spare box of good ol' black tea was located, and my heartrate was able to return to normal, safe in the knowledge that I had a proper milky cuppa in my hand.

Revenge on the Wire: Chapter Two

The unmistakable pre-waft of cigarette smoke covered clothes entered Sarah's office, closely followed by Adam Kennedy. Adam, in turn, appeared to be followed by the smell of liberally applied Lynx body spray, presumably an attempt to cover up the initial scent.

Adam was a younger guy, probably early twenties with a white checked shirt, pink tie and dark blue suit. His hair appeared to be almost entirely constructed of Brylcreem.

After my introduction to Adam, I wanted to get a sense of how much he knew about what had happened at the company and how aware he was of Heartbleed.

"So, Adam, Sarah gave me the information about the incident with the password resets earlier this week…" I was interrupted before I could finish my thoughts.

"There are five people supporting that company. None of them are the smartest, someone made a mistake and reset all the passwords. Simple. Sack them all and replace them with better people if one of them won't admit to it. That's what I'd do," Adam said smugly.

Sarah interjected, "It's not quite that simple Adam, we can't let everyone on that team go because someone may have made a mistake, we also don't know for sure that someone did make a mistake, that's why Parker is here."

"I think you're wasting your money on this whole investigation, quite frankly," Adam responded. "A bad thing happened, customer will get over it. Move on."

Sarah rolled her eyes. It was clear Adam was either being naive or simply didn't like a forensics investigator playing in his yard. Both are entirely typical responses from IT folks whose systems fall under investigation. They take it personally; they worry about their own jobs and feel like they are being judged. It was time to play mediator.

"Adam, if I may. I would agree that taken on its own the password reset event could be written off as a simple mistake. However, there have been a couple of incidents this week, the Readiwork issue with merit increases, is the other," I explained.

"That one is easy to explain, too," Adam responded. "The CEO, Philip Francis, is the only person in this company with an Active Directory password that doesn't expire. He got pissed off that he had to reset his password every 90 days like everyone else, so I had to make it never expiring. I've also seen his password. It's guessable. I'd imagine he uses it everywhere. You know what people are like. Someone guesses his password or sends him a phishing email, breaks into Readiwork, and messes around."

Adam's theory was not that revolutionary. The situation described with non-expiring passwords is more common than many would like to admit. Senior executives frequently get exceptions to security policies, the justification being that such execs are far too busy to deal with a password reset every 3 months, and that if they get locked out because they forget a newly changed password, the impact to their time would be too significant. Unfortunately, executives are the most likely people to be targeted by phishing in an organisation. It has also been my experience that executives who request such exceptions, do not take information security particularly seriously, and support for a security culture must come from the top down.

"That is useful information Adam, and you could well be right. Will you work with me to confirm your hypothesis?" I asked.

Adam slouched back in his chair.

"I would love to," he said, clearly lying, which only made me more excited to wind him up with an overly excitable and positive tone.

"Great, let's get to work!" I said jovially. "Oh, before we get going – Heartbleed, you got that covered here, right?"

"Of course. I support a bunch of companies; I saw the story about the vulnerability on the news and checked all the externally facing servers for it. I found one box at another company that was vulnerable, and switched it off until I applied the patch," Adam said, once again defaulting to his smug face.

It was actually a pretty positive response. He was aware of the seriousness of the vulnerability, and had checked for it on a bunch of servers that he was responsible for. He found one vulnerable machine and isolated it until it could be fixed. A solid response all round. Couldn't fault him on that one.

Sarah had arranged for us to set up camp in the office of an out of town executive. Philip Francis, the CEO, had his office next door. He was in the office, but glued to the phone, so I wasn't able to introduce myself, but I would want to talk to him at some point.

I'd started to develop an action plan. There were two things that I needed to answer to keep Remoteli happy. Could we figure out exactly the chain of events that lead to the mass password reset at the customer site? Secondly, could I determine root cause of the Readiwork HRIS strangeness?

The first question could likely be answered by evidence located on servers owned by Remoteli and their customer. The second question, would require interaction with Readiwork, the cloud based HRIS vendor.

I requested that Sarah provide me with contact information for the Remoteli account manager at Readiwork. She had warned me however, that given that Remoteli was a pretty small customer for Readiwork, it was unlikely that I'd get a response for a couple of days from them. Given this, a different angle might need to be pursued. I started down this road while Adam got set up.

I opened up the LinkedIn app on my phone and ran a quick search for 'Readiwork security', within a couple of seconds I'd discovered that myself and a member of the Readiwork security team, had a mutual connection. The connection was a guy I'd worked with closely for three years at a penetration testing company some five years prior. I had no qualms about reaching out and asking to be introduced.

I made the call, "Charlie, it's Parker – how the devil are you old chap?"

"Uh oh, I get nervous when I see it's you calling, I just assume that you've found my personal information on the dark web or something," Charlie jokingly responded.

Charlie was a good guy who often gave me a hard time about leaving the penetration testing field to work in investigations. After a quick discussion and update on each other's families, it was time to get down to business. I asked Charlie if he'd be able to introduce me to the LinkedIn connection at Readiwork.

"No problem," he said. "She's a really great person, and will be willing to help I'm sure. I did some pen testing for them a couple of years ago."

We ended the call and within a couple of minutes I was part of a group text conversation along with my old buddy Charlie and Olivia Spencer, who was a member of the technical security team at Readiwork. Charlie explained that I was doing a forensics investigation that crossed into the realm of Readiwork's product and would like to speak to someone on the security team. Olivia responded after about 15 minutes and told me to give her a call anytime. I wasted no time in taking the opportunity to connect.

"Hi Oliva, it's Parker, thank you for agreeing to talk with me."

Olivia explained her role on the security team at Readiwork. She was in charge of vulnerability management, essentially scanning all servers in the Readiwork environment for known bugs and driving them to remediation.

"So, you've been busy with Heartbleed I'd imagine," I asked, somewhat inconspicuously, but with a hidden serious purpose behind the question. I'd considered that Readiwork could have been vulnerable to Heartbleed. It was a cloud service with a fairly large footprint, and thus if it had been vulnerable, and the CEO was reusing passwords between Remoteli and Readiwork, it was possible that was angle for this investigation.

"It's been pretty hectic obviously, but thankfully we didn't fare too badly. Most things are behind a load balancer that runs a non-impacted version of the SSL library. We did have a couple of machines that were vulnerable. They ran a project tracking app, but fortunately nothing in our production environment was impacted," Olivia explained.

I began to fill Olivia in on the details of the incident I was investigating. Of course, the customer facing issue was something that Remoteli did not give me permission to disclose to Readiwork, so I kept the scope of my disclosure narrowed to Readiwork component of the investigation.

I explained how the automated emails included the 'my heartbleeds for you' text, and how this was something that lead me to believe the vulnerability was somehow in play here.

"Mmm...that is bizarre," Olivia pondered. "I will have to dig into this, I'll be able to figure out the sequence of events that led up to the merit increase rejection action based on logs, but now I'm all paranoid that we missed something in regards to Heartbleed."

We ended the call with Olivia promising to kick off the investigation on her side and to get back to me with log files and other information that might pertain. In the meantime, I turned my attention back to Adam, and the Remoteli systems,

"So, Adam. Walk me through what we've got here."

Adam gave me a virtual whistle-stop tour of Remoteli's IT environment. It was a proven formula. Microsoft Active Directory (AD) domain, a bunch of Windows machines connected to it and an application environment that had been custom developed. The AD servers were in the office, the application environment hosted in a collocated datacentre just down the road.

The way Remoteli did business, was to get a software agent installed in a customer's environment and have that connect back into the application environment. Therefore, one helpdesk agent employed by Remoteli was able to manage several customers from the in-house developed software, which ran in a web browser.

Most of the Remoteli employees that did the actual support work, were based in Bangalore, India.

Email was also hosted in-house, by way of a Microsoft Exchange server.

Remoteli's internet facing presence was limited to a marketing website hosted by a third party, Outlook Web Access, for remotely checking email and a Cisco VPN for remote access to the Remoteli internal network. Unfortunately, I was able to confirm the VPN did not mandate the use of multifactor authentication. I gave Adam a slap on the wrist for that one.

For all his strange odors, Adam had a pretty good understanding of his environment. He'd cut a few corners over the years it seemed, but given he wasn't able to dedicate his entire time to this one company, that was not to be unexpected.

The Remoteli custom application was integrated with the Active Directory for authentication.

"So, essentially, the only logging we have right now is when someone authenticates into Active Directory, that is recorded," Adam explained. "But we have no way of knowing what actions they took beyond that."

Adam had essentially just described how Remoteli was logging events that were logged by default, and nothing more, which is of course extremely frustrating, but extremely common and something we investigators must learn to think around.

"Do we know the exact time that the mass password reset occurred?" I asked.

"Yes, it was at 8:30am our time on Tuesday."

Adam pulled up a couple of screens on his laptop. He showed some data that had been provided by the impacted customer, including several thousand log entries that showed how an account called 'svc-remoteli' had triggered the many password resets. This account was a service account used by the Remoteli software agents to make changes to the customer environment. Service accounts are commonly used by applications, the problem is, that when adequate logging of their use is not available they mask the human identity behind them.

"So, let's start by pulling anything we can find for Tuesday morning, AD logs, VPN logs, firewall logs and seeing what we can cross correlate." Adam began working on the request, but had a slight hesitation.

"I've logged into the firewall maybe twice since I've been working here, I don't really know Cisco stuff that well, so I might struggle. It's one box that is both a firewall and a VPN," he said.

"It's okay, if you can get me in, I can pull the config and the logs," I responded.

Fortunately, Cisco networking gear was firmly in my wheelhouse and had been part of many previous investigations, because it was so prevalent around the world.

Adam's admission was slightly concerning, however. If he'd not spent much time in the Firewall it was unlikely that it was being maintained. Could it have been vulnerable to Heartbleed but slipped under the radar? This would be yet another question to ponder as we moved forward.

Revenge on the Wire: Chapter Three

Adam had started to open up more during our correlation of log files from various sources. I think he'd started to understand that the investigation was not about him. Instead, we just needed to get to the bottom of the events. In fact, he understood by him helping, he would probably end up getting more resources that might make his job even easier.

Adam handed me a USB stick containing the various log files sorted into an easy to digest folder structure. I added the log files to a new AccessData Forensic Toolkit case I'd created. This would be my official record of the files, and this action also ensured that checksums of the files were calculated. Checksums are used to prove that the files were not altered during the investigative process, critical if someone is to be prosecuted based on the data they include. We always go into an investigation holding evidence to this highest standard. If it's good enough for the law courts, it's good enough for anything else.

I took a copy of the AD logs and ran them through some bash shell commands on my laptop. I used 'grep' and regular expressions to filter out the usernames from the logs, and then sorted them alphabetically. The end result was a list of 40 or so unique accounts that were active in Remoteli's Active Directory environment the time of the mass password reset event.

Most of them were obviously accounts that belonged to specific people at the company, Remoteli was using a fairly typical first letter of first name followed by surname username format. There were also a couple of service accounts on the list.

"The service accounts here, this one looks like it's related to Exchange, and this one?" I said pointing to the list. One service account had a generic name 'access-acct', I wanted to be sure that Adam could explain sufficiently what it was. He could.

"Yeah, that guy is an AD account used by the VPN to authenticate VPN users through AD," he said.

"Ah, makes sense." I replied. "So, it's safe to say that of these 40 user accounts, people were active either in the office or on the VPN?" I asked, seeking confirmation.

"Correct."

I looked back over the list of accounts.

"I might need you to help me get a list of job roles and functions for these people," I mentioned to Adam. "Is that something you can do?"

"Yes, I can do that, I will just pull the data from Readiwork."

There was one noticeable omission from the list. The CEO, Philip Francis had not been logged in at the time of the mass password reset incident.

"So, Mr. Francis's non-expiring password wasn't used that morning, Adam."

"Uh, I guess not. That's a surprise."

That was an important discovery. A highly vulnerable and highly valuable account was not active at the time of a significant security incident. Maybe, just maybe, these two events were coincidental after all? It was entirely possible.

Adam had logged into the Readiwork system, and was copying and pasting job title data from that system into a spreadsheet and matching it up with the list of accounts that had been logged into AD that morning.

"Huh, they still have Patrick in here. Probably need to update that," he said to himself before turning back to me. "Okay, here is the list, most of the folks are helpdesk agents, of course. Couple of finance and a couple of HR, and one developer."

I thanked him for the list, but wanted to re-examine his previous comment.

"Who's Patrick?" I enquired.

"Huh?"

"You just said Patrick was still in Readiwork?"

"Oh. Patrick was the original founder of Remoteli, he left about two months ago. He was a good guy. A techie."

"And he's still in the HR system? Does he still work here at all?" I asked.

"No, he left for good, he's probably still in there since they might still be paying him a few months of severance or something."

"Does he still have an AD account?" I asked.

"Nope. They made me delete all of his accounts the day he left. He's out for good."

"Do you know why he left?"

"Uh, it was kinda strange. The story goes that he hired Philip Francis to help bring the company to the next level, and the two of them didn't get on so well, but the investors liked Philip more than Patrick, so Patrick had to leave," Adam explained. "The official story was that Patrick decided to leave to start a new company, but none of us have heard from him since."

The fact that they had recently lost a pretty key employee, a founder of the company, was somewhat alarming. It was additionally concerning that there were two versions of the same story. It's not uncommon for there to be a corporate spin on the story of a departure, for morale reasons, but still I made notes on what I'd just been told.

"What was Patrick's surname?" I asked Adam.

"Cappelli," He responded. "Patrick Cappelli."

I wrote down his name. It would be a name to follow up on for sure, but for right now the facts were that he was a former employee without network access, so he was not on top of the investigative priority list.

We turned our attention to another set of logs. This time from the Cisco VPN. These logs were more useful. They would allow us to further distil which of the forty users we knew were online that morning were in the office, and which were logged in remotely. The logs also included the public IP addresses from which those accounts were logged in from. This is useful, since public IP addresses can be tied back to rough geographic locations. So, at the very least, if you're not expecting people to login from Russia, and you have accesses from Russia, you know there might be an issue.

In this case, there were five people on the VPN out of the forty that morning, and all appeared logged in from British IP addresses. I confirmed they were all residential broadband connections, using an online whois lookup tool. Whois records tell you which organization is the registered owner of a domain name or IP address.

Nothing seemed problematic, but of course I recorded these findings for further analysis later.

While we'd been pulling logs from the Cisco VPN, I'd also taken a moment to pull down a copy of the firewall configuration. In Cisco speak, I'd executed the command 'show run', short for show running configuration, and placed the output into a text file. The resulting config file includes details regarding firewall rules, and other configuration parameters on the Cisco appliance. I decided to study this file next, but was interrupted by a phone call. It was Olivia, from the Readiwork security team.

"Hi Parker, I have some info for you that will probably be very useful," she announced. "Are you ready to copy?"

"Go right ahead."

"Well, first of all, on Heartbleed. I verified once again that there was absolutely no evidence of compromise on any of systems as a result of the vulnerability. The systems that were vulnerable were patched within a couple of hours, and even if they were compromised, would never have been able to get access to production."

"That's great, I appreciate you checking that out," I responded, acknowledging in my mind that the 'Philip Francis password compromised by Heartbleed' theory was all but done.

"On the actual action of rejecting the merit increases. I can confirm that it was done by the Philip Francis account, as expected. However, there are a couple of interesting things you should know about that account. It has a, erm… somewhat atypical history," Olivia explained.

"Huh, okay, go ahead - now I'm super interested," I responded.

"I'll email you all the details so you can see it up close, but from our audit logs I can tell that the Philip Francis account leveraged the Readiwork mobile app to make all the rejections that Remoteli saw."

"The mobile app?" I replied. "Interesting, I assume that he'd have had to login to the mobile app with the same username and password as your website, right?"

"Actually, no. And this is what I think you need to look into. Are you ready?" Olivia asked, ensuring that I had a couple of moments to focus entirely on what she was about to tell me.

"Yes, please go ahead."

"So the way our mobile app works is, we use Oauth tokens to authenticate the app into our platform. When you login to the app the first time, you get a token, which you can then use until it is revoked." Olivia explained.

Oauth is an authentication standard used typically used to authorise applications to access data from a given service. The standard leverages tokens that contain information about the scope of authorisation given.

"And how does a token get revoked?" I asked. "Is there a time limit? Do they expire?"

"Actually no, they never expire. They only get revoked if they are revoked manually, or if a person logs out of the mobile app."

This was a little odd to me, I would have expected there to be an expiration time, that would have kicked someone out the platform and forced them to login after a set time. A few months at the worst.

"And that token is only ever stored on the mobile device, correct?" I was quickly trying to remember how the Oauth authentication standard worked.

"Correct."

"Well, I need to look at Philip Francis's phone then," I said, thinking aloud. A stolen Oauth token from a phone? Unlikely, but a possibility.

"Erm. If you do that, you might be looking at the wrong phone." Olivia explained. I was confused.

"How so?"

"Well, remember how I said the account had an atypical history?"

"Yep."

"The user associated with this account wasn't always Philip Francis' account. Previously, it was named 'Patrick Cappelli', it seems as if they account was renamed earlier this year. There was another Philip Francis account at the same company that was deleted around the same time. The Oauth token issue date, predates the renaming of the account," Olivia stated.

"Okay, so what you saying is, that an account was renamed, and presumably repurposed in Readiwork. I was actually just made aware of the staff change that probably lead to that," I glanced at Adam. I paused and took a moment think through what I'd just heard. "So, when that account was renamed, can you tell if the password was reset?"

"I can. It was."

"Mmmm...and that Oauth token was not expired at the same time?!"

"It was not," Olivia's said sheepishly. "Before you say anything, I have filed a bug report. We should expire Oauth tokens when passwords are reset. We don't do that today."

I needed to draw out a quick timeline sketch to recap the conversation. So, I asked Olivia to hang on for a second while I talked through the events we'd just discussed, drawing and writing as I did.

"A couple of months prior to today, Remoteli asked Readiwork to rename an account from 'Patrick Cappelli' to 'Philip Francis'. You did that, and then reset the password for that account. However, you did not expire the existing Oauth token. Hence, there was another way into the account. A backdoor, through the mobile app, if you will."

"That is correct," Olivia replied.

"In which case. I think I need to have a conversation with Mr. Cappelli. Thank you so much for your help Olivia!"

We wrapped up the call. Olivia once again promised to send me a summarized report of what had occurred, along with supporting log files.

I needed to brief Sarah, so headed in the direction of her office. While doing so, I noticed the man I assumed to be Philip Francis, based on the nametag on the door, had now finished his phone call. I took the opportunity to introduce myself and pick up on a couple of details.

"I really hope you can get to the bottom this Mr. Foss. This has been a pretty shitty week for me," Philip said after I made my introduction.

His phone started to ring again. It had the unmistakable iPhone marimba ringtone known the world around.

"Before you answer that, one quick question, have you ever used the Readiwork mobile app?"

"No, never," He responded while beckoning me to leave.

"Thanks," I said as I headed through the door.

I fired off a quick text to Olivia.

"Are you able to tell what type of phone that token lives on, based on a user agent string or something?"

"Yes. Android device," came the response.

Revenge on the Wire: Chapter Four

I sat down with Sarah, and filled her in on my conversation with the Readiwork security team. I also let her know I'd picked up on some of the history in regards to Patrick Cappelli, and would be interested in the real story. As it turned out, it hadn't been an amicable split. There was an ongoing argument about how much severance Patrick was entitled to, and legal proceedings were about to be spun up on both sides.

"I remember what we did with Readiwork," Sarah explained. "We wanted Philip to have all the same permissions as Patrick, so we just reused Patrick's account. But we changed the password, to be safe."

"Unfortunately, doing so didn't log the account out of the mobile app on what I assume is Patrick's Android phone," I explained.

"He did have an Android," Sarah looked saddened. "So, you think Patrick is behind all of this?"

"Well, right now, we know he, or someone in possession of his phone definitely caused all of those Readiwork emails to come through. But on its own, that would seem pretty frivolous, so we need to dig in more here."

"Okay, I'll let Philip know."

I went back to the other office and took my seat next to Adam once again.

I needed to pick up where I'd left off. I was reviewing the firewall configuration when I'd had to take the call from Olivia at Readiwork.

It was a pretty easy to follow configuration. Poorly, although as is usually the case, most traffic was allowed to flow out of the office network. Traffic from the outside was markedly more limited. There were rules specific to the VPN and email services. Then I noticed a rule that was a little different.

It was a firewall rule that permitted access on any port to pass through the firewall, if that traffic was sourced through a specific IP address. I ran the IP through the whois tool. It again was a British residential broadband IP address. Without explanation, this was a highly insecure firewall rule. It was allowing unfettered access to all traffic from this one IP address, which presumably belonged to someone's house. There was another issue. The rule had been set to never log matching traffic. This meant anything connecting from that IP wouldn't show up in the firewall logs. It was designed for maximum stealth.

I highlighted the rule on my screen and asked Adam to take a look.

"You know what that rule is all about?"

Adam shook his head.

"No, that's crazy." He said.

I looked back at the list of IP addresses from the VPN logs I'd pulled earlier. None of those IP's were a match for the one in the rule, which figured, given the no log condition.

My phone pinged with an email. It was the consolidated data from Olivia at Readiwork. I opened it up on my laptop to check out the data on a larger screen. A collection of logs, along with a summarised report had been passed along.

Of most interest to me was an audit log file that showed the exact steps that had lead up to the moment the 'my heartbleeds for you' comment had been entered into Readiwork.

Unlike Remoteli, Readiwork had a pretty flawless logging game. Although cloud providers sometimes get a bad name when it comes to security, in this case, the level of detail in the logs might have just saved Remoteli from having to pay out a significant severance package. The reason, there was an IP address associated with the actions taken on the mobile app. You guessed it, that IP address matched perfectly with the IP address in the firewall rule.

"Tell me this Adam, did Patrick have access to the firewall when he was here?"

"Of course, he was the guy who set everything up. Literally everything," Adam responded.

In an investigation, we always look for means, motive and opportunity. It seemed Patrick, by virtue of a firewall rule that gave him access to do whatever he felt like in the Remoteli network, along with a mobile app that was preauthenticated into what had become Philip Francis' Readiwork account, gave him all the means required to be involved in both of the week's events. Secondly, a deepening rift between the current and former leaders of the company, which had financial implications for Patrick Cappelli provided motive. He wanted revenge. He wanted to cause problems for his former company. Major problems, like taking a large customer offline for a day. Heartbleed had provided the opportunity. By inserting a cryptic message into the Readiwork message about Heartbleed, he'd hoped that the vulnerability would be highlighted as the cause of the mass password reset. He probably also didn't think that a company that had previously skimped on IT spend would bother to bring in an independent investigator.

I wasn't done yet. Although it was looking increasingly likely Patrick Cappelli was responsible, I needed a firmer link to the mass password reset. A firewall rule alone, although shady, doesn't reset passwords. He still would have needed AD access, and his own account had been deleted.

"You know, Cappelli also set up the service account that the VPN uses to authenticate people. He probably knows that password," Adam piped up.

"And does that password have the ability to do anything other than authenticate users?" I asked.

"Let me check."

Adam leaned in and took a look at the security group memberships for the VPN service account.

"Shit. It's a domain admin." he said, with his face turning pale.

"Uh oh," I replied. "You know what that means. It can do whatever it wants."

A disgruntled former employee had full blown access to various systems that he knew wouldn't have been attributable to him.

His only mistake was entering the Readiwork system to create a diversion. He didn't know how detailed their logging was, and ultimately, it was that which lead us back to him.

It was time to contain the problem before it became worse.

The firewall rule was removed. All active VPN sessions were reset. All accounts in the active directory environment were validated and had passwords reset. The Oauth token was removed from Readiwork by the Readiwork security team. Logging was enabled and tickets were filed for auditability improvements in the Remoteli application.

"It always happens like this. It takes an incident, but once you have one, suddenly security becomes the priority," I said to Adam, patting him on the back. He was clearly upset at himself for having failed to double check some of these things previously.

Sarah called us both in to talk to Philip Francis. I briefed him on what we'd discovered.

"So, it's looking incredibly likely that Mr. Cappelli is doing this as an act of revenge against the company," I concluded.

"I'm not surprised he'd do something like this, the guy is getting desperate," Philip said. "This goes directly to the police right now, because quite frankly I'm worried about what he'll do next."

A police officer was summoned to the office and statements were taken. I would have to formalise my report and send it over to the police officer that evening. Materials were preserved, this one felt like it would almost certainly go to court. It was about as clear cut violation of the Computer Misuse Act as any that I'd ever worked on.

It was time for me to head back to the lab and start on the report. Philip Francis pulled me aside as I left.

"Of course, the only thing worse than a service provider making a mistake, is a service provider getting breached. I've got a lot of thinking to do about whether or not we disclose this to the customer. So, remember that NDA you signed if you go to down a couple of pints tonight, okay."

I understood the predicament that he was in. Tell the customer it wasn't a mistake and deal with the fallout from the breach notification, which in many ways could be worse, or just continue to peddle the line that an employee had made a mistake and foot the bill. These are the reasons I'm glad I'm not a CEO. Tough call.

"Well, my only piece of advice would be this. If you take this guy to court, I promise you this story is interesting enough it'll end up in the papers. And you can count on me not to disclose anything Mr. Francis. In this game, reputation is everything. Have a good night." We both nodded and went our separate ways. There was one final person waiting to talk to me. Cigarette in hand, leaning against a purple Ford Escort, it was Adam.

"Thanks for today buddy. I found that to be a pretty interesting day of work," he said, his tone completely different from the one he'd adopted when we first met. "I thought that you needed extremely fancy gear to do this type of work, but really you just used tools that I use every day for the most part. Got me thinking maybe I could do this type of work one day."

"The customer doesn't care about the tools, the customer cares about the result," I explained. "In the end, all this work often requires that you be a second pair of eyes, or think about things from an outsider's perspective. It also helps when your mate knows someone in the security team at the cloud service you're working with."

It was a good point. Connections were important. Had Olivia not been connected with Charlie; I could have been still waiting to get someone at Readiwork to respond.

"Have a good night Adam, I will see you around."

Finally, it was time to head out.

Revenge on the Wire: Epilogue

Selfishly, it was the best kind of court case. Other than modifying my report into statement format there wasn't much for me to do. The police were able to use the evidence collected to establish probable cause and get a search warrant. They seized Patrick Cappelli's phone and computers and performed their own forensics based on my earlier work.

The phone had the matching Oauth token on it. The computer had evidence of connections into the Remoteli firewall.

Patrick Cappelli plead guilty, and was sentenced to 18 months in prison.

Remoteli decided to disclose to its customer that they'd had a security breach based on a previous employee still having systems access. The customer was not impressed.

They demanded refunds and suspended their contract with Remoteli. This cost Remoteli around half a million quid. Ouch.

If that wasn't bad enough, Remoteli was also forced to rebrand and change names because as predicted, the story ended up in the papers and a couple of other customers walked away from their contracts, too.

Readiwork made changes, as promised, and made all Oauth tokens expire in their environment when passwords were changed.

Cappelli was a father of two, and you always reflect for a moment when your work leads to a person being incarcerated, or financially damaged.

However, ultimately, we're all responsible for our own actions. I've worked on multiple cases involving vengeful former employees. It's not worth the effort, quite frankly, to involve yourself in such a mess. Move on, and live your life.

I do occasional work with Adam these days. I offered him an apprenticeship on the condition that he stops smoking and starts using real cologne. He's proving to be quite the agile resource.

Perhaps best of all, he lives in Slough, so I can use him instead of having to go there myself. Perfect.